CONSPIRACY

ISLAND

Robert Deslauriers

ISBN-13: 978-1-7772042-2-8

To my beloved wife. You captivate, inspire and motivate.

I truly would be lost without you.

CHAPTER 1

"Beep...beep...beep..." Gabriel smacked the alarm to turn it off and rubbed his eyes. It was still dark out, so he took a minute to get his bearings. He's not a morning person at all and normally enjoyed sleeping in. On this particular morning though, he was getting up a little early to get some fishing in while it was still a good time. The fog in his head started to clear as he sat up and looked at the clock again. 6:05 am. He sighed and contemplated crawling back under the covers and forgetting about the fish. "Just get in the shower," he told himself. The hot water cascading down his body was very soothing. It was like he was thawing out after being frozen in a block of ice.

After showering he started to feel alive again and made himself some coffee along with hot cereal. He quickly gobbled the food down, and then poured the rest of the coffee in a tall steel thermos to take with him. Peering out the window at the lake, he noticed the sun was starting to peek over the horizon. What a nice, calm morning. There wasn't even a breath of wind - perfect. The thermometer outside revealed a cool 10 degrees Celsius. Once the sun got higher it would quickly get warmer, likely over 20 degrees. It had been a fairly cold spring, which wasn't necessarily unusual for Northwestern Ontario, Canada. It was now the month of June. The ice had just disappeared from the lake a few weeks earlier.

Gabriel grabbed some chocolate bars to snack on, threw on his warm coat, laced up his boots and headed out the door. He had built his house at the edge of a secluded lake. Gabriel enjoyed having quiet, peaceful surroundings, and Robson Lake provided that. His was the only house built there and he had bought much of the property around to ensure that he could retain privacy for some time to come. It's not that he was anti-social, though he was a quiet man. He had grown up in a rural setting and sometimes felt a little awkward trying to carry on a conversation. Plus he enjoyed hunting and fishing so it made sense that he would have a place out in the middle of nowhere. The nearest town was Fort Frances, where he traveled to get groceries and supplies once or maybe twice a month. He kept those trips to a minimum because it took about an hour to drive there. This kind of life was enjoyable for him, though it also made him lonely at times.

Outside the house a large Akita dog quickly ran over to see Gabriel. Nick was a fine companion and helped with the loneliness Gabriel felt at times. Akitas are known for being friendly and very intelligent. One thing Gabriel really liked about them is that they are also known for being tenacious sometimes. For example, his grandfather's dogs had chased a large black bear up a tree once. Living by himself out in the bush, Gabriel wanted that kind of dog that would protect him and his home.

"Good morning Nick. How are you today? Want to go for a boat ride?"

Nick yelped excitedly. He knew what those words meant. Nick always jumped at the chance of going for a boat ride with his master. The two headed down to the dock and Nick jumped into the boat, panting loudly and bouncing around. Gabriel untied the boat and tossed the lines in. After putting on his life vest, he stepped over to the steering controls and fired up the four-stroke jet motor. He bought this motor because he tired of having to worry about the prop getting chewed up on some rocks in shallow water. After letting the motor warm up for a bit, Gabriel slowly pulled away from his dock. The water was just like glass. Nick was looking at himself in it as they moved, making Gabriel wonder whether or not he knew it was his reflection. Once he got out in the open water he cranked the throttle open most of the way causing the shore to rush past with a blur.

After a few minutes Gabriel noticed another boat ahead and off to the right. He slowed to about half speed and turned toward the other boat. He recognized it as John Edberg's. Gabriel slowed down even more now so that he could say hello, but he couldn't see John. Carefully, he eased up beside and looked into the boat, cutting the motor. Everything looked fine except for the fact that no one was inside. Keeping a hand on John's boat Gabriel scanned the surrounding water but saw nothing on the surface. He told Nick to stay and stepped onto John's boat after tying the two together. He looked at everything but found nothing suspicious. There was plenty of fuel, the paddles were still on board and the emergency kit was in place. The motor started up just fine. Why would the boat be drifting in the middle of the lake?

"Maybe he got out onshore and the boat slipped away," he thought to himself.

Gabriel yelled loudly, "John! Can you hear me?" The only response was the echo of his call as it rolled across the water in the clear morning air. Gabriel looked at the surrounding shoreline for any movements. As he scanned slowly, his eye caught something. He froze, trying to focus his eyes. There it was again. Just a slight motion, but Gabriel couldn't make out what was moving. The object was about 500 yards away from him so he pulled his mini binoculars from his pocket and trained them on the shore. As he focused the lenses, he saw the source of motion. It was a moose at the edge of the water staring back at him curiously. His shoulders fell along with his hope. He remained there looking around with his binoculars for another ten minutes when he finally realized that nothing would be seen from there.

Gabriel put his binoculars away and grabbed a spare rope from John's equipment. He tied one end to the bow of John's boat and tossed the remainder into his own. Next he lifted John's motor out of the water to make it easier to tow and also to prevent any possible damage to the prop. Then, after stepping back onto his boat he secured the other end of the rope to his stern, allowing enough slack to safely tow John's empty vessel. After shoving away, Gabriel started his motor and slowly started toward the shore nearby. He thought about just taking it home but realized he'd never forgive himself if he later found out John was on shore and needed help.

Once Gabriel was within 50 yards from shore he turned to run parallel so that he could look closely at the rocky beach. Robson Lake had a few nice sandy beaches but it was mostly rock. The nice thing with this lake was that the water was very clear, making it easy to see at least 50 feet down. So while Gabriel looked closely at the rocky shore he also glanced into the water in case there was anything at the bottom.

He kept trolling along, following the twisting shoreline. After about a half hour he saw the outline of the upper half of a body on the rocks. The person had dark clothes on so he blended in well. Gabriel called again as he approached.

"John? Is that you? Can you hear me?"

He feared the worst when the person did not respond. Gabriel carefully pulled his boat to shore, shut off the motor and jumped out. He ran over and gently turned the body over. It was definitely John. Looking at his face Gabriel realized that he had been dead for a while, at least a day. He checked for a pulse anyway. Maybe it was just his emotions running away on him but he couldn't help thinking that maybe there was something he could do. When there was no pulse found, Gabriel just sat and stared at the lifeless body of his friend. He sat there for a good ten minutes before he realized that his feet were numb from soaking in the cold water from the lake. It shocked him back to reality and he stood up out of the water. Gabriel cautiously pulled John's body up onto the shore out of the water and set it down. Then he kicked himself. The police would need to analyze the area. Maybe he shouldn't have moved the body. He sighed and decided to go back home towing

John's boat with him and phone the police, leaving the body there.

Gabriel called Nick over and told him to stay to guard the body from any animals that might come along. Nick sat obediently and Gabriel boarded his boat to leave. He used a paddle to shove John's boat away, then he pushed off a rock in the water to get his boat free and sat down. The motor came to life with the turn of a key and Gabriel turned to leave, with Nick watching him. He moved along as quickly as he safely could towing the second boat. On the ride home he couldn't stop thinking about John and what might have happened. There had not been any storms recently so that could not be the cause. What could have made John fall overboard? Maybe he slipped on something? But there was nothing on the floor that would have done that. Perhaps it was a heart attack or something like that? But John was a young man, around forty years old. He also had a healthy lifestyle. However, Gabriel remembered hearing of an athlete dying suddenly of a heart attack when he was only near thirty. It could be that was the cause.

As Gabriel neared his dock he had settled on the idea that John had a heart attack and fell overboard and drowned, washing up on shore. He slowly pulled up to the dock and tied his boat off, then John's. Before he turned to go into his house he started unbuckling his life vest. All of a sudden a light bulb went on: John's body didn't have a life vest on. Gabriel knew John was always very careful when boating and particular about having a vest on at all times. Some people didn't take this matter very seriously but John was almost overly particular about this.

Gabriel went back to John's boat and looked again. He couldn't see a vest anywhere. He stepped inside to look under everything and inside the bins, but there was not a life vest to be seen. He stepped onto the dock again, tossed his vest into his boat, and then slowly walked up toward the house. He was reviewing the scene of John's body in his mind. There was no life vest on John and nothing close-by. Gabriel had not seen one floating near the boat when he found it either. John's vest was a bright orange color so it would have been clearly visible.

Gabriel was now very suspicious about his heart attack theory and about the whole situation. He climbed up the stairs to his large deck and took off his wet boots to dry in the sunlight. When he got inside he headed to the phone and dialled the local police.

CHAPTER 2

Constable Nicole Edouard of the Ontario Provincial Police (O.P.P.) was sitting at her desk complaining of boredom to her partner Frank Hauser when her phone rang. She quickly grabbed it and answered.

"Constable Edouard here," she said.

"Hello, I need to report something. Can I talk to you about it?"

"Yes, sir. Please explain the situation."

"I found the body of a friend of mine washed up on shore not far from my home. He's dead."

"Ok. I'm sorry to hear that. Could I get your name sir?" Nicole responded.

"Yes, it's Gabriel Johnson."

"Where do you live Mr. Johnson?"

"I'm about an hour from town. You can take Highway 11 east of the Fort and then turn up Highway 502. My driveway is about 30 kilometers north. I'll go down and set up a marker for you there."

"And you say this is your house, or a cabin?"

"It's a year-round residence."

Nicole raised her eyebrows and shook her head in disbelief. She knew that there were cabins all over the place in this region but hadn't come across any permanent homes in the area Gabriel lived. She thought he must be a hermit or something.

"Alright sir, we will get ready and head your way within an hour or so. I guess we won't reach you until after noon. We'll need you there to ask you more questions and to show us where the body is."

"That's fine," replied Gabriel. "I'll see you in a couple of hours."

Nicole hung up the phone and looked at her partner with a grin.

"So much for being bored today," she said. "Not only do we have a dead body to examine, we also get to visit a hermit!"

"That should make for an interesting afternoon," Frank replied.

"Do you want to round everyone up while I get the car and a coffee for the drive?" she asked.

"Only if you get me a coffee too," he stated with a grin.

Frank made a few calls and packed up the gear he and Nicole would need. He went outside just in time to see Nicole pull up with two coffees and their lunches.

"Is everything ready to go?" she asked him.

"Yup. The guys should be around with the boat any minute."

A white pickup truck with blue decals pasted all over it saying, "Police" and "O.P.P." appeared. It was towing the O.P.P. boat and had a couple more officers inside. Behind was a white van with similar decals, being driven by the medical examiner.

"Good, let's go," Nicole said excitedly. She was happy to get out of the office to do something. It was turning out to be such a beautiful day.

*   *   *

At around 1:00 pm the police finally found Gabriel's driveway. It was just a simple, winding gravel road. But as they drove deeper Nicole started to appreciate the beauty of the spot. This part of the country was very rugged. The Canadian Shield terrain is full of exposed bedrock, lakes, forests, and swamps. Gabriel's driveway was rugged but lined with tall beautiful white pine trees growing naturally. Though it was a very long driveway, its prettiness made the drive worthwhile.

"There is a house in here right?" Frank asked.

"It must be here. The sign at the highway pointed this way."

When Nicole was starting to second guess herself, the trees and bush started to thin out and a lake became visible. Then they saw the house. It was not what either one expected. It was like a dream home. Gabriel had built right on top of a large piece of exposed bedrock. The house had two levels with a large wooden deck that wrapped around from the side to the front, facing the water. On the water side, there were large picture windows that gave a breathtaking view of the surroundings. It had been built out of stone and large wooden beams. It looked like it belonged in Europe with the stone cottages they are famous for. It matched the forest and lake wonderfully. Nicole felt embarrassed about her comments on the way there. She had somehow imagined it would be a rundown shack that a demented old man lived in.

She pulled up to the house and parked near the three-bay garage that obviously was also a workshop. It too had been built from stone. She noticed a wood shed tucked in behind the house. Gabriel clearly had a wood furnace and liked to keep busy around his home. The yard was immaculate.

"You survived the drive," said Gabriel as he came out from the house.

"Yes. We were starting to wonder if you were trying to get us lost though," replied Nicole.

Gabriel smiled nervously and looked down at his feet. Nicole was a gorgeous brunette. She was also fairly tall, just under six feet. Pretty women made him awkward and self-conscious. "Uh, please come in," he told her.

Nicole was struck by Gabriel as well. He was tall, over six feet, with dark features. He was a ruggedly handsome man. Under his clothes she could tell he was well built, likely from all the time spent outdoors chopping wood and doing other chores. She was caught off guard, again because she expected someone far different.

"I'm Constable Edouard and this is my partner Constable Hauser."

"Nice to meet you," Gabriel responded shaking hands. "I'm Gabriel."

"Mr. Johnson, would it be ok with you if the other officers in the truck there put the boat in using your landing?" Nicole asked.

"Oh yes, that's no problem. If it's alright with you, please just call me Gabriel."

"Ok," she said.

Nicole and Frank stepped inside while the other policemen backed the boat to the water. Inside the house both of them noticed the same meticulous care that was evident outside. Gabriel's home was spacious yet uncluttered and clean. The living room and dining room enjoyed the view of the lake. The floor was walnut hardwood in the living room and dining area. It was mostly brown but with some red flares throughout. The living room had a large leather sofa and a leather reclining chair. There was a vaulted ceiling above. On the one side of the living room was a nice set of mahogany hardwood stairs leading to the second floor. That floor overlooked the living and dining rooms with a rail running the length of the two rooms on the wall opposite the windows. Behind the rail was a walkway to the bedrooms, where a person could stop to look out the windows or talk to someone in the living area. Above the kitchen at the end of the second floor walkway was a rather impressive library. Nicole was amazed by the wooden bookcases inserted into the walls holding hundreds of books.

She looked back at the main floor and saw that the kitchen had gorgeous wooden cupboards stained a dark rich cherry color. Gabriel had put in slate tile on the floor which extended over to the door. There was a fridge, dishwasher, gas stove, microwave and enough storage space in the cupboards to satisfy any woman. On the one side there was a small walk-in pantry. Between the dining room and kitchen there was an island with three chairs and the sink. The countertops were made from granite. The place had the look of a cabin with all the wood, but the colors on the walls and lighting kept everything bright, evoking a warm, happy feeling. In behind the kitchen area was more space which Nicole guessed was for a bathroom and laundry room. Nicole took a look at the table in the dining room. It had four chairs. What impressed her was the intricate carving in the wood.

"Where did you get this table?" she inquired.

"I had it shipped over from Thailand actually. I went there a couple of years ago and toured the King's wood carving school. They have all kinds of things there you can buy. Anyway, I saw this table and thought it would cost a small fortune. Actually, the price was no more than you would pay over here for a solid wood table without any carving, and that included shipping. So I bought it and had them ship it here. It was a bit of a pain to get in the house but I love it."

"It's very impressive. In fact, this whole house is incredible," she said.

"Thanks."

Nicole's first impression of Gabriel was that he had good taste and was clean and particular about his home. He showed a certain amount of confidence but at the same time there was a shyness to him.

Often when he spoke he would look her and Frank in the eye, but other times he would look down like he wasn't sure of what to say. He even blushed a little when she complimented him on his home. He seemed kind, gentle and innocent. Nicole was usually a very good judge of character, and even though she tried to be very careful not to make quick judgments in her work, she felt as though Gabriel had nothing to hide.

Frank jumped in and said, "Do you think you could tell us about how you found the body?"

"Sure. I was up early to go fishing. When I headed out on the lake I found John's boat which I towed back here and tied to my dock as you can see."

Gabriel walked over to the window and pointed at the boat.

"Before I came back, though, I looked all around for John. I couldn't see him at first so I checked everything in the boat and it seemed fine so I just thought maybe he was onshore and the boat got away from him. I tied it to my boat and drove along the shoreline for a while when…when I saw his body. When I checked, it was obvious he had been dead…"

Gabriel went silent and looked at the floor. Frank and Nicole looked at each other and waited for him to gather his composure. Seeing John dead was hitting Gabriel hard now. It was starting to sink in that he was really gone.

"Sorry," Gabriel mumbled. "John had been dead for a while already. I left the body there with my dog and came back here to phone you."

"You left your dog?" Frank asked with his eyebrow raised.

"Ya, I thought it would be good to guard the body from animals."

"Uh-huh," Frank replied.

Gabriel was starting to feel like an idiot when Nicole reassured him, "That's ok. I imagine there are a lot of bears around here so it's probably good you did that."

Nicole inquired, "How did you know the man?"

"His name is John Edberg. He comes fishing here fairly often. I've known him for a few years. Actually, I met him when I built the house here about five years ago."

"Did he use your landing?" asked Frank.

"No, there's a landing of sorts further down the highway. It's pretty rough but some people use it. I guess John's vehicle would still be there."

"Does John have any relatives that you know of?" Nicole wanted to know.

"Yes, he's married. I don't really know his wife very well. Her name is Wanda. I think John's parents live out west somewhere. I've never met them."

"Would you mind taking us to the body now?" Nicole requested politely.

Gabriel grabbed his jacket and some fresh shoes. They stepped outside and started down toward the dock.

On the dock Gabriel stepped onto his boat. The two officers and medical examiner with the O.P.P. boat were ready to go and waiting inside their boat. Nicole asked Frank to examine John's boat while she went with Gabriel.

"Eye, eye, captain," Frank said with a hint of sarcasm.

Nicole just smiled at him and jumped into Gabriel's boat. Gabriel went to his bin and pulled out an extra life vest for her.

"Thank you," she said as she took it from him.

"You're welcome." Gabriel looked down a bit again.

Gabriel put on his own vest and started the motor. As he pulled away from the dock he couldn't help but look again at Nicole. She was sitting in front of him looking straight ahead. From the moment she arrived Gabriel had been smitten. She looked to be in her early thirties. Even under her uniform Gabriel could tell she had a slim, attractive build. Her eyes were green, and he noticed some natural highlights that stood out in her brown hair when the sun's rays hit it. Her face was pretty, particularly when she smiled and revealed her perfect teeth. This was the kind of woman that Gabriel liked and he promised himself to be careful around her. Usually he embarrassed easily around pretty girls, and often felt as though he could never say the right thing and felt stupid. Deep down he hoped he could do something to impress her and maybe she would show an interest in him.

"There's no way a girl like that is going to look at you," a voice from within scolded. "Don't even entertain the idea!"

While all of this was raging inside, Gabriel drove to where the body was and found Nick faithfully waiting for him. Both boats eased up to shore. The other two officers went with the examiner to the body.

"Was this how you found him?" the examiner asked.

"Actually, his legs were in the water and he was lying on his stomach. I pulled him out and flipped him over."

Nick came bounding over to Gabriel and he commended his dog for being obedient.

Nicole asked, "What's his name?"

"Nick."

Nicole gave him a pet and said hello then asked, "Is there anything else about finding the body that you can tell us?"

"Well, I don't know if you'll find it significant but there is one thing that bothers me about this whole situation. There's no life vest on John and he always made certain that he and anyone in his boat had one on."

"Hmm. Maybe it came off in the boat somehow," she said.

"Actually I checked and it's not there and I didn't see it anywhere around here when I was searching."

Nicole turned to the officers and asked them if they would look around for a vest while they were compiling evidence. She turned back to Gabriel and asked, "Could you take me to where you found the boat while they do this?"

Gabriel got Nick to hop in and turned the boat around. He went back to the spot he remembered finding John's boat. After turning off the motor, he looked at Nicole while she scanned the area. She could not see anything that would be useful to the investigation so she asked Gabriel to take her back to the body.

When they pulled up, Nicole walked over to John's lifeless body and asked what the officers had found. There wasn't much to say. The body had no suspicious markings on it and there was nothing around the body to help explain what happened. It looked like an easy case of a man falling out of the boat without a vest and drowning. A search of the area turned up nothing. They found his wallet and car keys in his pockets and that was it. Once all the initial investigating was done they loaded the body into the O.P.P. boat and drove back to Gabriel's house.

Nicole asked Frank, "Did you find anything?"

"Nothing. The boat looks fine. There's nothing to indicate how the man died. There is a little blood but it could just be from fish or a cut. It looks old. I grabbed a sample anyway."

"Did you happen to find a life vest?" she asked next.

"Nope."

Nicole took a deep breath. The air was fresh and clean but she still felt a little disturbed by this case. It appeared that John simply drowned but

Gabriel's comment about the life vest bothered her. She questioned whether she could trust him. If John had simply drowned, what purpose would it serve for Gabriel to lie about the life vest? If Gabriel had killed John, why would he try to raise suspicions by bringing up the life vest when everything seemed to point to an accidental drowning? It didn't make sense. So far, she felt she had no choice but to accept what Gabriel said.

Nicole made a request, "I hate to bother you some more Gabriel but could you show us how to get to that landing John would have used?"

"No trouble at all," he replied.

Nicole turned to the other boat and said, "We'll see you back at the office."

The officers and examiner nodded and started removing the body to prepare to leave. Nicole, Frank, and Gabriel got into the O.P.P. cruiser and started down the driveway. When they drove into the landing they saw a half ton pickup parked with a boat trailer behind it.

"That's John's truck," said Gabriel.

The group parked and got out. While Frank and Nicole looked in the truck, Gabriel walked to the lake and looked around. He couldn't see any life vests and was disappointed that there were no other boats around either. Dejected, he walked back to the police car and waited for Frank and Nicole to finish. They found nothing beneficial in the truck.

"Well I guess I could take this and load up the boat to take back to the station," Frank stated.

"Not much else we can do here," agreed Nicole.

He started the truck up using the keys that had been on John's body and Nicole got into the car and drove Gabriel home.

Nicole got out with him and said, "Thank you for your help today. We'll contact you if we need any more information. In the meantime, if you think of anything, here's my card. Just give me a call, ok?"

"Ok. Thank you."

Gabriel watched the car disappear into the trees. He went inside his home and plopped down onto his leather chair in the living room. It was suppertime but he didn't feel like eating. He got up to pour himself a scotch then sat down again, replaying the day in his mind. After a while he turned on the TV to see what was on. He didn't feel like thinking anymore.

CHAPTER 3

Wanda Edberg invited Nicole and Frank inside her home in the town of Fort Frances. She seemed a little startled to have two police officers at her house.

"Can I offer you some coffee or tea?" Wanda asked.

"No thanks Mrs. Edberg," replied Nicole. "We actually have some sad news."

Nicole proceeded to explain about John as gently as she could. Wanda looked stunned. She turned away from them and started to cry. They waited a moment and then tried to ask a few questions.

Frank went first. "Mrs. Edberg, when was the last time you saw your husband?"

"He left yesterday morning. He told me he was going out to do some fishing and that he might stopover somewhere for the night."

"Do you know where he was planning to stop or what lake he was going to?

"No. I usually don't ask where he's fishing because I don't know where the lakes are anyway.

He has a number of friends with cabins and sometimes he will stay with them, especially if the lake he's going to is far from town. Maybe I should have asked, but he's gone so much in the summer with guys fishing that I just stopped asking questions years ago. Where did you find him…his body I mean?"

"He was at Robson Lake. Do you know a man named Gabriel Johnson?"

"Yes, we've met. I think John went fishing with him sometimes. Is that lake near his house?"

"Yes, that's right. He found your husband."

Nicole asked, "Did your husband have any health problems?"

"He got sick sometimes but everyone does. He didn't have any major problems if that's what you mean. His health was actually pretty good."

"He never had blackouts or anything like that?"

"No, not that I know of."

"What line of work was he in?"

"He's a mechanic at the dealership just down the street."

"What about you? What do you do for work?"

"I work for a gem company. I help with getting mineral rights to property where prospectors find gold or any other precious metals."

"Does that keep both of you pretty busy?"

"It's ok. We're usually home for the evenings and had weekends off."

"Could you provide us with the names of his fishing buddies so we can see if they know anything more?"

Wanda proceeded to list off all the friends she could think of. Afterward, Frank and Nicole looked at each other, out of questions for now. They thanked her and expressed their condolences. As they walked out the door, Nicole stopped and turned around. "Did your husband take a life vest with him when he left?"

"I don't know. I suppose he did. I think he usually had one."

Wanda looked a little confused by the question, as did Frank.

"Thank you. Good night Mrs. Edberg."

As the two walked away Frank asked Nicole: "What's with the life vest?"

"It's just something Gabriel said. It probably doesn't matter anyway. Don't worry about it."

Nicole pretended to shrug it off but she still couldn't help thinking about what Gabriel told her. They got into the car and started driving back to the station. After calling all of John's friends they got no additional information. Nicole decided to go home. It had been a long day and she needed some rest.

*   *   *

The next morning Nicole finished the paperwork she could do then checked in with the medical examiner for some results.

"What can you tell me today?" Nicole inquired.

"Not much. Mr. Edberg's death was caused by drowning. That's not a surprise. There were no signs of trauma on his body. There's nothing to indicate this was not an accident."

"Did he have a heart attack or something like that?"

"No. It appears that he just fell in for some reason and drowned."

"Thank you Doctor."

Nicole turned to walk away and as she headed back to her desk she decided to close the case as an accidental drowning. It looked like John just failed to have his vest on for some reason and it cost him his life. She headed to the coffee room to fill up her mug before she finished her report. On the way, a tall strong man named Jack Rudiger stopped her. Jack looked like a man in his forties, though he was over fifty. He worked hard to keep himself in shape and was proud of it. He stood at about six feet four inches, and with his heavy build he could intimidate most people. Jack served as the detachment supervisor so he would check up on all the cases from time to time.

"How is the Edberg case coming Constable Edouard?"

"It looks like an accidental drowning sir. I was just headed to finish up the paperwork."

"There is no evidence to suggest foul play?"

"No sir. We checked over the scene and the guys looked at his boat and vehicle carefully. We talked to his wife and coworkers and friends, but nothing indicates that this was a murder. The body is clean and the examiner is certain that drowning was the cause of death."

"Ok, it sounds like you covered your bases Constable. Thank you."

"Yes sir."

Jack quickly left, obviously on a mission to pick on someone else. Nicole was glad to get that over with. She detested going over cases with Jack. He seemed pleasant enough but she never cared much for him. She finished getting her coffee and went to her desk.

CHAPTER 4

As the sun began to set west of Gabriel's home, he sat on his deck pondering the fate of his friend, John. A couple of days had passed since he found the body and Gabriel heard that they were ruling it an accident. He never would have thought that this would happen to someone he knew. It was hard to accept the reality that he would never see John again. Death never is easy to adjust to.

Gabriel stood up and went into his home to grab a flashlight. He wanted to go for a walk along the shore and knew it would be getting dark soon. Nick tagged along as Gabriel slowly made his way around the bay. As the light gradually faded he stopped to sit on a stump and stroked Nick's head. In a few minutes, all light from the sun disappeared. The moon provided enough to see a short distance so Gabriel didn't bother turning his light on just yet. He slapped at the mosquitoes biting him and then remembered why he usually did not go wandering around much at dusk. The bugs were usually particularly bad around that time.

He stood up to walk back home when Nick started to act strangely. He was whining and growling as he looked across the lake. Gabriel stared in the same direction until he spotted what was troubling Nick. All thoughts about the mosquitoes disappeared from his mind as he examined an island toward the far end of the lake. It was too far to be able to distinguish what was going on but he could see the beams of flashlights as people walked around.

"Come on Nick. Let's go home."

Gabriel started making his way back but kept his flashlight off. He could make out the shoreline in the dim moonlight, plus he felt nervous about the people on that island. He didn't want them knowing he was there. Part way home the island disappeared from sight behind the wandering shore. Because he knew he would be out of view the rest of the way Gabriel turned on his light and hurried along. He had never seen anyone on that island and the fact that someone was there at night raised his suspicions. Who would be there at this time? What were they up to? He wanted to check it out.

Gabriel tied up Nick and said goodbye then went down to the boat and cast off. He started the motor and slowly idled into the lake. He left his running lights off so that he could sneak up to the island. There were no worries in his mind because he knew the waters here. He was completely confident that he could navigate in the dark. By keeping a slow pace the motor remained very quiet, virtually undetectable at a distance. The new four-strokes were so much quieter than the old two-stroke motors. Once he was about half-way there, he stopped the motor and tried to discern what was taking place. It was now so dark that he felt safe from being spotted.

He pulled out some night vision binoculars that he brought along. He had bought them because he thought they would be cool to have and occasionally checked out animals in the yard at night. There were at least three people on the island wandering around. It looked like they might be carrying something to the boat tied up to a dock at the edge of the island. The distance was too great to make out exactly what was going on. Gabriel was debating whether he should get closer but he didn't want them to spot him. One more look through the binoculars was all it took to convince him not to go any further. One of the men turned slightly, just enough to reveal a rifle. Gabriel knew that they were not just camping on the island at that point. It was time to get help.

Gabriel wanted to bolt as fast as he could but he knew that too much speed would give him away. He held his breath as he started the motor again. His eyes were fixed on the island. He was imagining them hearing his boat and firing at him with a flurry of bullets. But nothing happened. They could not see or hear him. Gently, he eased the throttle forward and carved through the water back to his home.

After what seemed like an eternity, he pulled up to his dock and raced into the house to his phone. Right beside was the card Nicole had given him. Looking at the clock he noticed it was now 10:00pm. He hesitated for a moment but decided to call Nicole anyway. He dialled her cell phone number and after two rings she picked up saying, "Hello?"

"Hi Constable Edouard, this is Gabriel Johnson. I'm sorry to call you at this hour. Is it a bad time?"

"No, not at all. I'm usually up at this time. What can I do for you?"

"I just saw something that I think is suspicious. I was out for a walk when it was getting dark and noticed some flashlights out on an island here. I have never seen anyone out there and thought it was strange to see this at night. So I boated out about half-way there to get a look at them. I'm not sure what they were doing but I saw one of them holding a rifle."

Nicole sat up a little straighter in her chair. "Are you sure it was a rifle?"

"Yes, I'm certain."

"Did you say it was dark already when you saw this?"

"Yes, but I was looking through night-vision binoculars."

"You have night-vision binoculars? Where did you get those?"

"Um, well, they're just something I got for fun. Anyway, I could see the gun clearly with them."

Nicole paused and decided to forget about the binoculars. "Do you know if anyone owns the property on that island?"

"It's Crown land."

Nicole thought for a moment. It did seem strange that there would be people out there with a rifle. "I'll come out right away," she finally decided. She hung up and called Frank.

"Hi Nicole, what's up?"

"I just got a call from Gabriel Johnson. It sounds like there is some suspicious activity out by his place."

"What do you mean?" Frank inquired.

"He said that he saw some guys on an island and one of them was carrying a rifle. I thought that it was worth checking out."

"That's an hour drive. If they aren't shooting at anything then it might just be some guys camping and they brought a rifle in case of bears or something."

Nicole replied, "I suppose that's possible. Nonetheless I would like to check it out. Something about this feels funny."

"Well I'm not going along. It's after work hours anyway. Have fun chasing campers around an island."

"Ok Frank, but when I arrest them I'll get all the credit!"

Frank just laughed and hung up. Nicole grabbed her gear and headed out the door, bound for Gabriel's. She made pretty good time getting to Robson Lake. As soon as she pulled up, Gabriel came out to meet her and they went to the boat. He showed her where the spotlight was and explained that he would go slowly without lights on so as not to attract attention.

"I don't want to confront anyone right now. Let's just take a look from a distance," Nicole instructed.

They trolled out to the place Gabriel had stopped before and Nicole took a look through Gabriel's binoculars. She had seen the flashlights as they approached and now a closer examination revealed two people carrying some indistinguishable items and one person holding a rifle. She whispered to Gabriel to get closer. He nervously shut off the motor and paddled his boat to within a hundred yards of the island while Nicole kept her vision focused on the three strange people. She was still trying to figure out what was taking place when the one holding the rifle turned and stared in their direction. She whispered at Gabriel to stay still and looked back at the gunman. He was still turned toward them. Could he see them? Had he heard them approaching?

His head turned to the others, obviously saying something to them. They quickly disappeared from view. However, the gunman remained in his position, watching carefully. It seemed like he knew someone was there but just couldn't make out their position. Neither party was willing to move for the next few minutes, until suddenly the other two men reappeared and dashed toward their boat at shore. Bullets began to puncture the water's surface close by, followed by the sound of automatic gunfire as it echoed across the lake.

"Go, go, go!" Nicole ordered. Gabriel didn't hesitate. A second later they were flying across the lake. Gabriel kept the lights off and jetted along what he knew to be safe waters. Meanwhile, the three men started their pursuit in the direction of the engine noise. One man started to scan with a spotlight as they drove. The high-speed chase in darkness was frightening for Gabriel and Nicole. She was unsure of this man's abilities and realized her life was now in the hands of an untrained civilian. She did not like losing control like this but what choice did she have?

Gabriel was trying very hard to control the rate of his heartbeat but was barely succeeding. His chest felt like it was going to burst and his hands began to tremor like someone with Parkinson's disease. As they raced along he tried to keep track of where they were in relation to shore. He knew where to go. Not far ahead there was a narrow opening in the shore that would lead to another arm of the lake. The narrows are quite shallow and normally anyone passing through would need to go very slowly while someone in the bow directed them away from rocky parts. To attempt passage at night was risky, but

Gabriel had the jet motor that could handle shallow areas and he also knew what places to avoid.

Gabriel yelled to Nicole over the noise of the motor and wind roaring past. "Turn on the light and aim it at the shore on the right side. We're looking for a twenty foot opening."

Nicole understood. She started searching for the narrows but immediately after switching on the light their pursuers opened fire. Bullets tore into the water just to the left of them. Gabriel swerved away and then the opening he was hunting for came into view. As they made for the entrance to the narrows, another burst of gunfire erupted and bullets sailed past them. Gabriel's boat disappeared from view as he started to navigate the shallow water. He slowed to the fastest pace he dared take. Nicole was praying that he knew what he was doing as he veered left and right through the rocky waters. It took them about thirty seconds to escape the narrows into the opening deep lake. Gabriel circled around to face the mouth of the slim stretch of water from the side, out of view. Next he cut the motor and told Nicole to turn out the light.

Gabriel explained his plan as they waited. "Chances are they don't know their way through the narrows and with the speed they're driving they'll wreck their boat for sure. If they make it through then they will likely drive right past us so we can either surprise them or double back and get to safety."

"Ok, works for me," she replied. She couldn't help but be impressed at his quick thinking under the stressful circumstances. They waited together in the darkness as they heard the other boat enter the dangerous passage. The driver slowed down some but felt confident driving straight since the other boat had obviously made it through quickly. It wasn't long before the propeller hit a rock. The motor screamed as it jerked, launching the propeller up out of the water. It splashed back down only to hit another rock, this time shearing the propeller clear off the base of the motor. The driver hit the kill switch but it was too late, the damage was done.

A moment later there was more screeching, like the intense scream coming from the wheels of a braking train. The bottom of the boat slammed into a large boulder beneath the surface. All three men were thrown to the floor. Gabriel couldn't help but grin at the sound of the crash. His plan had worked, but now came the dangerous part.

The three men could be heard for miles, yelling at one another over the damage done. When they saw the battered motor one man slapped the driver and complained about his incompetence. If they had stopped arguing for a moment they might have been able to hear the idle of Gabriel's motor approaching. Using their lights as a guide, he was slowly making his way to them, like a serpent cautiously slithering near to its prey. Nicole had decided to sneak up in the dark while the men made their noise. When they were close enough Gabriel flicked on the light while Nicole trained her sidearm on the man with the rifle. She ordered them to drop any weapons and put their hands in the air. The men froze for a moment, then the gunman tried to take a quick shot, but he was not fast enough. Nicole fired twice, hitting her mark each time. The man fell hard onto the edge of the boat, flinging his rifle into the lake.

Nicole repeated her order and this time they complied. She told them to kneel with their hands on their head and they obeyed. Gabriel used a paddle to pull alongside and Nicole carefully stepped across to the other boat. After searching for weapons she handcuffed one man then tied the other one with some rope. The one she shot had not moved. She checked for a pulse but he was dead. Nicole lowered her head and took in a deep breath. Even though she killed him to protect herself and Gabriel, it still bothered her to be responsible for the loss of a life. This was the part of the job that disturbed her sleep at night.

Leaving the dead body where it fell, Nicole forced the other two men into Gabriel's boat. After sitting them down in the bow where she could keep an eye on them, she asked Gabriel if he could tow the other boat back with them. It took a bit of work but Gabriel managed to push the boat off the large boulder underneath by using his paddle for leverage. He tied the boats together so that the other one would trail behind at a safe distance. Nicole scanned the water with the flashlight hoping to spot the rifle that had been dropped in. It was nowhere to be seen. They would have to return in the daytime to find it. With all the lights on they started their return home.

Upon arrival, Nicole made the two sullen men walk up to her car and put them in the back. They had not said a word since their capture. Gabriel untied Nick and commanded him to keep an eye on the two in the car. He sat and watched obediently. With them secure, Nicole used Gabriel's phone to call Frank.

"Hi, Frank. Did I wake you?"

"Yes, as a matter of fact," was the groggy reply.

"Well I need you alert. You're going to have to meet me at Gabriel's. I have one dead body and two live ones under arrest."

"What? What happened?"

"I'll explain it all when you get out here. See you in an hour?"

"Ya, ok, I'm coming."

Gabriel invited her to sit in the living room and try to relax. "Would you like some tea?" he asked.

"Yes, that would be lovely," she told him. She sat down heavily on his leather couch and reviewed the night's events in her mind while Gabriel started a kettle in the kitchen. On the drive there she had not imagined facing the scenario the two had entered. She still was amazed at Gabriel's response out on the lake. She looked at him admiringly while he got the tea ready. Nicole was starting to find this man to be very intriguing. How many people could effectively handle such an intense situation? He was proving to be much more than she initially estimated. She caught herself, though. She did not want to get too close.

With the tea ready Gabriel turned to head to the living room and Nicole quickly looked away. He handed her a mug and sat down on the chair opposite her seat. "Is police work always this exciting?" he asked her with a slight chuckle.

Nicole just laughed. "Maybe in the city, but here it is usually fairly quiet with bigger problems occurring from time to time." She set down her mug on the coffee table and got up to look at her car. Nick was still watching the two men inside, and they appeared to be uncomfortable with him staring. She smiled at the thought of grilling them once she got them back to the station.

Turning back she asked, "What do you think they were doing out there anyway?"

"I have no idea. It's a fairly big island so they could have been trying to hide something or maybe there is something on it that they want. Either way I can't imagine what would be so important to them."

"How big is it?"

"Oh, it's probably about eighty acres. I've never really wandered around on it but it looks like it has quite a few trees."

The two of them continued tossing ideas back and forth of what might be out there while they waited for Frank. Once he arrived, Nicole filled him in on the night's events. They loaded up the dead body and Nicole said goodbye to Gabriel before making the trip back to town.

CHAPTER 5

Despite the late night, Nicole was up early and had the two suspects put into separate interrogation rooms. Frank came and told her that they were ready to go.

"Did they ask for their lawyers?" she inquired.

"No, they haven't said a thing."

"Ok, I'll see if I can get them to talk."

Nicole started with the driver of the boat. When she walked into the room he didn't look up at her. She sat and stared at him, but he didn't budge. "Do you want to explain why you assaulted me last night?" she asked.

The man didn't move.

"Look at me!" she commanded.

He raised his eyes and glared at her.

"I don't like being shot at and I want to know what you and your pals were up to last night! If you don't start talking it'll just make things more difficult for you." Nicole was seething. But the man just smirked at her and looked back at the floor, saying nothing. She wanted to reach across and throttle him. She kept throwing out questions and threats, but he said nothing. Frustrated, she walked out slamming the door and the man started to grin again.

Nicole met with the same results when she questioned the other man. Realizing that she would get nowhere, she had both of them put back in their cells and went to her desk. The only way she was going to get any information would be to figure out what was on that island. She grabbed Frank and checked to see if they could take the company boat. However, the boat was occupied for the day, so Nicole called Gabriel and asked if he could chauffeur them around the lake once more.

On the drive Frank apologized for not going with her the night before. He felt terrible that she had to face three guys on her own. But, as always, Nicole had come out on top. When they arrived, Gabriel was ready and he took the two of them out on the lake. He pulled up to the island at the spot the others had parked the night before.

"Alright, the men were carrying something into the trees there but we didn't see where they put it," Nicole informed Frank. "Maybe if we fan out and search we might find a clue."

"Did the boys at the station find anything in that boat we confiscated last night?" Frank asked.

"Nothing but blood so far."

"I'll head around the left side if you want," he offered.

Nicole agreed and told him, "We'll work around the right and come back through the center."

Gabriel and Nicole spread out a bit to look for any signs of activity. Gabriel could see footprints for a little while but they disappeared at a rocky patch and he couldn't find any more. All three wandered around the island for the afternoon but they could not find any hints about what those men were doing there. The only signs left behind were a few footprints closer to shore where they parked. They were puzzled by this whole situation. Nicole was losing hope of solving this case. Frustrated, they climbed back into the boat and drove to the narrows to find the rifle that had been thrown into the water.

*   *   *

Back at the police station the two criminals were pacing in their cells, situated side by side. Neither one had said a word since their arrest. Both of them were caught off guard when an explosion rocked the building. They were slammed to the ground and pelted with rocks, cement and dirt. Coughing on the dust searing their lungs, they looked up at the giant hole that had been blown out of the wall. It was just large enough for the occupants of their cells to escape. Masked men jumped inside and jerked them to their feet, dragging them out the hole before any guards could respond. Once outside, they ran to a nearby van with blacked-out windows. The two were thrown in the back and the van took off, its engine screaming as they disappeared around the corner. By the time the police figured out what had happened, the van was long gone.

*   *   *

When Frank, Nicole and Gabriel returned to the dock, Nicole decided to check in with Jack

Rudiger. She was met with an angry voice. "Hello sir. Is everything alright?"

"No, it's not. We were just attacked!"

"What happened?" Nicole asked anxiously.

"Somebody just blew up the wall where those two idiots you found last night were locked up! They escaped and nobody seems to know what happened or where they went. Where are you?"

"Oh no. We're out at Robson Lake. Frank and I were searching for some clues on the island and we also grabbed the rifle that the dead one dropped when I shot him."

"Did you find anything there?"

"No sir. All we have is the rifle."

"I need you here to help figure out what went wrong."

"Yes sir, but what about Gabriel?"

"Who?"

"Mr. Johnson…the one who helped me last night. Isn't he in danger now with those two guys loose? They know where he lives and they saw his face."

"Yes, that's right," Jack said slowly. "Change of plans. You and Frank stay out there for the night and keep watch. We'll sort this mess out here without you. I'll touch base with you tomorrow and decide what to do from there."

"I understand, sir. Goodbye."

Nicole hung up the phone and looked at Gabriel and Frank. Both of them heard her mention Gabriel's name and wanted to know what was happening.

"The two men we arrested last night just escaped custody," Nicole slowly explained. She did not want Gabriel to panic so she left out some of the details. "Frank and I have been ordered to spend the night here with you just in case there are any problems. They probably won't come back, but we'll be here in case."

Gabriel stared out the window blankly. He couldn't believe this was happening. Would they really want to do something to him? It was impossible to know. Was there really something on that island that would be valuable enough to kill him for? Both Frank and Nicole could see that Gabriel was not taking the news very well, and they couldn't blame him. Who would ever think that this could happen?

Nicole pulled Frank aside and quietly explained all the details to him. "Explosion? Do they know how or who did it?" Frank asked impatiently.

"Shhh. No, they don't. Rudiger said that he'd contact us again tomorrow. They might know something by then. For now, we have to keep watch."

Frank and Nicole set up a plan for watching the house and tried to help Gabriel keep his mind off the potential threat on his life. Nicole wandered the grounds in the afternoon and got a better look at Gabriel's place. In behind the kitchen there was a nice size laundry room with a new front-loading washer and dryer set. At the back end of the house he had a wood furnace that ran the heat for the winter. Outside, hidden from view behind the house was a wood shed, right by the back door for easy access. Most of the wood was gone by now of course so she knew Gabriel would be spending a lot of time this summer chopping up more firewood. Not far from the shed was a small greenhouse. Looking inside she could tell that he had already started some vegetables growing in there.

Walking up to the garage she could see through the window that there was an ATV, likely used for hauling wood. There was also a medium sized tractor with a snow blade sitting behind it. With the size of his driveway Gabriel needed to have a good plow. Next to the tractor sat a new 4x4 quad cab pickup truck. It looked like there was an empty bay, maybe where he parked his boat for the winter. In behind everything was an assortment of tools and equipment all neatly arranged on shelves and work benches. Nicole was getting a good picture of what kind of man Gabriel was. He obviously had enough money to live comfortably. He liked to keep himself busy around home gardening, cutting firewood, and caring for other maintenance. He liked the outdoors and having privacy. She could also tell that he was particular about keeping things neat and tidy. Gabriel was certainly not a typical bachelor. Nicole was discovering there was much more to this man than an initial glimpse provides. To her, he was becoming… desirable.

Back inside, Gabriel had started to cook supper. "I hope you like pasta," he stated to Nicole when she came in.

"Yes I do. Actually I'm a big fan of Italian food. What are you making?"

"Just a simple dish. Spaghetti with meat sauce. I hope you guys don't mind moose meat. I hunt, so most of my meat is wild."

"That's fine," both replied.

"Can I help you?" Nicole offered.

"Sure, you can watch the spaghetti while I work on the sauce."

"What kind of sauce do you use?"

"It's my own recipe. I like to add the spices myself. The store-bought sauce just isn't the same as homemade."

Nicole thought to herself, "The man can cook too. What are his flaws? He can't be perfect."

The two continued working together on supper while Frank kept an eye out for any danger. After supper, Nicole told Frank that if he wanted to catch some sleep she would take the first night shift. He was quite happy to accommodate and Gabriel showed him to the spare bedroom upstairs. When Gabriel came back down he finished loading the dishwasher and sat down with Nicole.

"What happens tomorrow?" he wanted to know.

"We don't know yet. Our supervising officer will contact us with more directions and we'll go from there. Don't worry, though. I'll make sure you're taken care of."

"If you don't catch those guys soon I don't imagine you'll be able to spend too much time watching me. What happens after a week or two, or a month?"

"Try not to think about it ok? Just focus on one day at a time and let us worry about those criminals."

Gabriel tried to fake a smile and stood up. Before he started to get ready for bed he asked if she needed anything. He told her to help herself to the kitchen if she wanted anything and said good night. Going into his room, he shut the door and sat down hard on the bed. He wasn't going to sleep much, but he climbed under the covers anyway and closed his eyes. All he could see, though, was those men coming into his house after him. It was not going to be a restful night.

CHAPTER 6

Nicole woke up Frank at about two o'clock in the morning. It was his turn to keep watch. He jumped out of bed and rubbed his eyes.

"Is there any coffee down there?" he wanted to know.

"You owe me. I just made a fresh batch for you. It's been quiet all night. There's a fog on the water too so you'll have to watch that carefully."

"Ok. I'm on the job."

Nicole was happy to close her eyes for a while. She went to sleep quickly. Frank poured a coffee and sat near the windows for a look outside. Over the next few hours Frank emptied the pot trying to stay awake. Just when light started to trickle across the sky as the sun approached, Frank got up to make more coffee. He loaded everything up and walked back to the window to wait. The fog was starting to fade with the sunlight filtering across the water. Frank looked over to the dog house to see Nick up, looking at the lake. He started to bark and growl. Frank wasn't sure if there was an animal nearby, or if Nick just liked to make noise, but he kept his eyes focused on the disappearing fog just in case. There didn't seem to be anything there. He looked back at Nick for a minute. The dog was getting very agitated and growling even more loudly. Frank turned his head back again but saw nothing.

Both Gabriel and Nicole heard the dog and woke up. Gabriel knew that something was wrong, but before either of them came out of the bedrooms there was another sound. It sent shivers down their spines when they heard the shattering of glass on one of the windows, followed by a heavy thud. Nicole grabbed her gun and carefully opened her door. She could see the broken window. Staying low to the floor she peeked over the balcony and there was Frank, on the floor. She called to him but he didn't move. Gabriel poked his head out the door next to Nicole and turned white when he saw her gun drawn.

"Come with me!" she commanded. "Stay behind me."

The two carefully headed down the stairs. There was more shattering glass as bullets whizzed by, just missing them. They jumped down away from the windows and the shooting stopped. Nicole briefly lifted her head to look outside and saw that a boat had emerged from the fog and was approaching. They didn't have much time before it would reach the dock. The dog was going crazy after the gunfire, barking and yelping. Nicole crawled over to Frank. There was no pulse. She wanted to cry but knew that she couldn't under the circumstances. It was more important for her and Gabriel to escape than to grieve right now.

"Come on, Gabriel! We have to get out of here! Let's go out the back door. They can't see it from the dock."

"How are we going to get away without them catching us?"

"They can see my car, but they can't see your truck. Let's go to the garage."

Quickly, they ran to the back door, staying close to the floor. Slipping outside, Nicole scanned the area looking for threats. The way was clear. They bolted across the yard to the garage and closed the door behind them.

"We have to move fast," Nicole told Gabriel. He ran to the shelves and grabbed a few large bags and threw them into the back of his truck. They jumped in and he fired up the engine while the large door opened. As soon as the door cleared the truck roof, Gabriel stomped on the accelerator. The goons in the boat were just getting onto the dock when they heard the roar of the truck. They started shooting as Gabriel and Nicole passed by. A few bullets hit the vehicle but did nothing that would stop them. Nicole looked behind as they raced down the driveway and saw the annoyed face of one of the men she had tried to interrogate. He couldn't shoot, though, because they quickly disappeared into the bush down the winding driveway.

When the end of the driveway came into view Gabriel stopped abruptly. Up ahead at the highway there were two SUVs and a truck parked, with men standing beside, waiting. It looked like they were pinned between the killers. Gabriel made a snap decision. He thrust the truck into four wheel drive and turned off the driveway to the left. He was following a very rough quad trail through the bush. The truck leaped and jerked as he drove over the aggressive terrain. He winced at the sound of trees scraping the paint on the side. This trail was normally used for gathering wood but now he hoped it would help them escape. The truck was now behind them following on the terrible trail. The men were being jostled around like rag dolls as they tried to gain on Gabriel.

The trail forked ahead and Gabriel turned to the right to head back towards the highway. The tires started flinging mud as he carefully made his way through a swampy section. The only reason he made it through was because of the 4x4. The trees cleared ahead and they shot out of the bush and into the ditch by the highway. He climbed up the side and took off heading north on the pavement. The tires were shooting mud all over the road as he sped away. The two SUVs weren't far behind him once they saw where he came out. The truck in the bush slid across the mud and slammed into a tree. The driver smacked the steering wheel then backed up to get out onto the highway. By the time he did, Gabriel and the SUVs already had a good head start.

Gabriel was pushing his truck to go faster than he ever had, trying to get some distance between him and the assassins. He knew that he would have to get off the highway if he was ever going to get away from them. When Cedar Narrows road appeared to the left he slowed just enough to make the turn and started down the logging road. The vehicles behind kept up their pursuit, but they were in for the ride of their life. Gabriel knew this road well from hunting. It was all gravel and consisted of a never-ending maze of twists and turns as it snaked its way west and north around lakes and swamps. The local logging industry had built the road to haul wood into the pulp and paper mill in Fort Frances. It was reasonably well maintained so the large pulp trucks could haul in and out, but it was still a bumpy ride and with all the hills and twists it was hard to drive very fast on it. Many who weren't used to the road would get motion sickness. In addition, there were many other smaller roads connected to it so there was a good chance they could turn off somewhere and hide for a while. Gabriel hoped to be able to get out of view long enough to break off.

Shortly after pulling onto the road, Gabriel grabbed his CB radio and announced that one half-ton was coming into the entrance from the highway. Every two kilometers, a sign would be posted with the mileage from the highway. Truckers would call out their location when they spotted a sign and state whether they were headed in or out. That way they would hopefully avoid any accidents as the road did tend to remain narrow. Gabriel had found the radio useful anytime he traveled the road so that he could pull over for any trucks coming. The truckers appreciated small vehicles letting them know they were there because they would often stay tight to the inside of corners and drive very quickly to make good time.

Gabriel was driving as fast as he safely could, which was making Nicole very nervous. She tried not to show it, but it was hard to hide when Gabriel would come ripping around a tight corner just barely keeping control. A call came over the radio that a fully loaded truck was coming toward them at the forty kilometer marking. They would likely meet him half way. Gabriel watched in the mirror as the three dark vehicles tried to keep up with him. Just ahead there was a steep hill down and back up again with a lake on the right. At the peak of the hill there was a hidden hairpin turn. Gabriel knew how fast he could go so he flew down the hill then took his foot off the gas, allowing their momentum to push them up the other side. As he approached the turn he gave the truck just enough throttle to go into the curve with the right speed, and he accelerated once he pulled through. Behind him, the first SUV was trying to make up time and failed to slow down enough. By the time they got to the top of the hill and saw how sharp the turn was, it was too late. The driver hit the brakes and cranked the wheel, trying to make it around the corner. But he ended up spinning out of control and flew over the side, bouncing off the steep embankment before splashing into the water.

The other two vehicles slowed down for the turn and avoided the fate of their colleague. Glancing down quickly, they saw the vehicle sink out of sight in the dark water. It didn't stop them. They kept up the chase. By now, Gabriel had gained a little on them and they needed to catch up. Both drivers were being more cautious, though, so they had a hard time closing the gap. For a few kilometers they could not even see Gabriel's vehicle, just the dust he raised.

When Gabriel passed the eighteen kilometer marking he called it out and the trucker responded with his own mileage report. He was at the twenty. They would meet in one kilometer. When they were almost there, Gabriel pulled over to the shoulder and announced to the trucker that he would wait there for him to pass. The trucker appeared shortly after and passed by without slowing down much, which was exactly what Gabriel wanted.

"Thank you, sir," said the trucker over the CB.

Gabriel stayed there to watch the truck as it approached the corner behind them.

"What are you doing?" asked a frantic Nicole. "We should keep going!"

"Just hang on. You'll see in a minute."

The truck driver was not expecting anyone else on the road because the people chasing Gabriel didn't have radios. Because Gabriel pulled over for him, the driver was almost going as fast as the road allowed. When he turned into the corner he cut it off by going into the oncoming lane. Half way through, he met the other SUV chasing Gabriel. The truck driver slammed down on the brakes and turned sharply to the right and the SUV driver did the same. However, it didn't prevent a collision. The large pulp truck plowed into the SUV and turned it sideways, then flipped it over and over as the truck tried to slow down. With all the weight of a full load of logs in the back pushing, the momentum was too great to stop. The SUV continued being pushed and flipped until it was crushed into a large piece of exposed bedrock on the roadside. It was completely flattened by the heavy logging truck, sparking an explosion when the gas tank was punctured. Flames shot out from underneath the vehicles and blew chunks of the SUV into the air.

The truck's trailer still had momentum and it tilted over, taking the cab with it as it began to spin. It was flinging logs all over the road. The driver of the last remaining vehicle chasing Gabriel, had just barely managed to slow enough to throw the vehicle into reverse and get out of the way. All three men in the pickup truck looked in horror at the scene before them. The flying logs, metal, flames and debris looked like a mini war zone. When the logging truck finally came to rest, the SUV looked like a small piece of burned scrap metal and tires. The road was littered with logs and the large pulp truck was hideously twisted and smashed, lying on its side. One of the trucks tires was in flames. It was probably just a matter of time before the large diesel tanks would erupt.

Gabriel's pickup appeared on the other side of the wreckage. He had turned around after they heard the crash. Both he and Nicole felt a little sick at what lay before them. They felt particularly bad about the pulp truck driver. Gabriel hoped that by some miracle he was still alive. Looking across the mess on the road, he saw that his problems were not over. The pickup truck started trying to get over to them. Gabriel turned around and floored the accelerator again.

"Those guys don't give up do they?" he muttered.

With 4x4 the pursuers managed to go into the ditch on one side and hop over a few logs in the way to push past the accident scene. Popping up over the other side they got back onto the road and took off after Gabriel. The chase continued for another half hour or so, with Gabriel managing to lengthen the distance between him and the hooligans. His dust trail was starting to disappear and they knew once that happened he could easily lose them on one of the side roads. Gabriel came to another fork in the road, the one he was waiting for. The main road continued to the left but Lost Axe Road led to the right. He turned to the right and headed in search of a hiding spot. He knew this particular area well from past hunting trips. As he and Nicole made their way along, behind them the men giving chase had stopped at the fork to decide which way to go. There was no dust, and both roads had recently been traveled, with the left road obviously looking more traveled and better maintained. They decided to go left, hoping that Gabriel would have stayed on the main drag a little longer.

Lost Axe Road was narrower than Cedar Narrows Road. They were still hauling some wood out on it so it was still getting some maintenance. Smaller roads branched off of it here and there but

Gabriel stayed on Lost Axe. Once they passed the last fresh cut block, the road quickly turned bad. No one maintained it past that point and it was clear that the rest of the road was from an old cut area. Gabriel had to slow down considerably thanks to large potholes and washouts.

Gabriel explained to Nicole, "Out here, once they stop repairing the roads it doesn't take long for nature to reclaim them. Within ten years the trees and bush will grow in on it. Vines start growing across and storms wash out the gravel. Often you wouldn't even know there was once a road unless you had been here before."

"Do you think they're still behind us?" she asked.

"I can't tell. There are a lot of little roads branching off up here so there's a good chance we lost them and they'll spend a long time searching for us. At the end of this road I know a spot where we can hide for a while and there's a nice lake we can use there too."

Nicole checked her cell phone.

"We won't get any service up here," he informed her. The phone was useless for the time being.

After what seemed like an eternity to Nicole, they finally saw an end in sight. They headed down into a ravine and back up the steep slope on the other side. From the top of the hill she could see another fork ahead. The road turned into swamp to the left and to the right the bush was closing in on the road making it impassable with a vehicle. Gabriel pulled right up to the fork and turned around then drove back up to the top of the hill he was just on. Nicole looked at him inquisitively, wondering what he was up to.

Noticing her look he explained, "Just in case they come down here I want it to look like whoever drove in turned around and went back out. You'll notice where we are now the road is rocky so they won't see our tracks turning off."

He pulled off the road and followed the bedrock for a short distance. Nicole could see a beautiful lake in front of them. The rock started to disappear as they headed downhill and turned to the right. Now they were driving on some long grass. The road behind them disappeared, and as they descended Nicole started to notice patches of gravel. They were driving on an old road that was hidden from view atop the hill. No one would see their tracks in the grass or even know that a road was back there. Gabriel followed the path for a short distance, enough to get completely out of view and hide in the trees, and then he parked.

Both of them sank down in their chairs and exhaled a large breath. It felt like they had been holding their breath the whole time on their hair-raising journey into the wilderness of Northwestern Ontario. They both seemed to be at a loss for words. Now they had to wait until it was safe to return.

CHAPTER 7

Nicole was the one that finally broke the silence while they waited in the truck. "So, where have you taken me?" she inquired with her eyebrow raised.

Gabriel grinned at her. "You make it sound like I abducted you or something."

"Did you?" she asked sarcastically. Both of them laughed nervously. The day's ordeal had left them exhausted and now their nerves were trying to recover.

"This is Carlton Lake. My dad used to bring me here fishing and hunting years ago. The hunting wasn't very good for some reason. There was lots of sign but we just had a hard time getting any moose into view. But the fishing is spectacular. Not many people came here, probably because the road wasn't that great. Plus, it was a good workout trying to get the boat down to the water. We used to carry it down on our shoulders from the road…but it made for some good memories."

Gabriel looked down and went quiet again. It was plain that he missed his father. Nicole hesitated to ask about him but couldn't help it.

"Where is your family?"

"My parents died a few years ago, before I built the house. They were in a car accident with my younger brother and all of them died. A drunk driver crossed the line and hit them head on."

"I'm sorry," she said.

"It was a long time ago."

It looked like it wasn't easy for him to talk about it so Nicole decided to change the subject.

"What kind of fish are in this lake?"

Gabriel perked up again. "We used to go for lake trout. There's also some large pike in there. This is a good time of year to go actually because the water's still cold. The trout are higher and easier to catch and both they and pike are feisty around this time."

"You know, I've never been fishing."

"What? Really? Did you grow up here?"

"No. I was raised near Toronto. My family prefers city life."

"Oh. Do you prefer the city too?"

"Not at all. That's actually why I was happy to come here. There's so much noise and crime in the city. Out here it's quieter and people are nicer. I kind of like the small-town atmosphere."

"Well…if you want, I can teach you to fish. I tossed a couple of rods in the back when we were in the garage."

"I completely forgot about that with the chase. What is in those bags you grabbed?"

"I packed a few things a while ago that I could grab in case of an emergency. I wanted to have some necessities ready in case I had to get away quickly, you know, if there was a forest fire or something like that."

"So, what do we have then?"

"There are a few liters of water and some tablets to clean any other water we might need to collect. I put in hand sanitizer, a first aid kit, fishing rods and some tackle, knives, beef jerky and other packaged food, and a bunch of other stuff."

Nicole hopped out and climbed into the box to look at everything. She also noticed a small tent,

flares, some clothes, matches and lighters, a compass
- pretty much everything someone would need to
survive in the bush for a few days. They were set for
now.

Gabriel walked back and said, "That tent is
pretty small. I wasn't really planning for much
company but if you wanted to sleep in it instead of
the truck I'm sure it would be a little more
comfortable. Both of us would fit in it but we'd
probably be cuddling…"

Nicole stopped moving. Gabriel started to
back peddle.

"Not that that would be a bad thing. I mean,
I'm not suggesting we cuddle… Wait, that didn't
come out right. Uh…" Gabriel stammered and
stuttered for a bit longer and Nicole just let him keep
struggling while a small smirk began to grow on her
face. Finally, he gave up trying to explain and walked
back to the door and jumped in the truck.

Nicole was laughing quietly. She couldn't
help it. He was just such a nice man and was trying
to help, but couldn't seem to find the right words
around her. She could tell that he liked her but was

too shy to say so at this point. She put everything back in the bags and climbed into the cab again.

"Don't worry about it," she told him with a smile. He turned an even darker shade of red and looked away.

After a few more awkward minutes had passed, Nicole's stomach groaned loudly. Gabriel's stomach also groaned, as if in reply to Nicole's. Both of them realized that they hadn't eaten yet and the day was almost over.

"Why don't we break open some of that food," Gabriel suggested. He got out and lowered the tailgate for them to sit on. Digging around in the bags, he looked at the tent again and glared at it. He didn't dare say anything about setting it up again. He would wait for her to ask. Bringing a few packages with him he sat down beside her and tore open a bag of jerky, offering her the first piece. They sat in silence, eating their jerky and granola bars while they watched the sun begin to descend.

"Would you like the tent set up?" Gabriel finally blurted nervously.

"That's ok. It's late and I think I'll be fine in the cab. It doesn't bother me for us both to be in there. But if you want to sleep in the tent then go ahead."

"I'll maybe just lean the chair back in the truck. You can lie on the back seat if you want."

"Sounds fair," she replied. "Isn't that sunset beautiful?"

"It is. I'm glad we're watching it together…" Gabriel felt like he had put his foot in his mouth again so he added, "You know, I mean, I'm glad that we're alive to see it. But I like being together with you watching it…" He gritted his teeth, trying to think of how to dig his way out of this one.

Nicole just leaned over, kissed him on the cheek and put her arm around him. Gabriel was a good man. He had saved her life more than once so far. Who could fault him for being a little tongue-tied around a pretty woman? She thought it was cute and wanted to reassure him. Her peck on the cheek did just that. Though he was thoroughly embarrassed and turned red again, he felt good inside. For once, he seemed to have the attention of a woman he liked. Too bad it was under such terrible circumstances.

They sat together until the sunlight was almost gone and the bugs began to get unbearable. Nicole curled up on the backseat with a blanket that was in one of the emergency bags. Gabriel leaned his seat back enough to snooze and they said goodnight.

CHAPTER 8

"Come on, Dylan. That guy obviously knows where to hide up here. I don't think we're going to find him." One of the goons in the truck searching for Gabriel said this to the driver. They had spent the night parked, trying to sleep. Now that it was daytime again, they were back on the prowl searching for any sign of Gabriel and Nicole. Dylan wasn't ready to give up just yet.

"I told you, we just need to find some gas so we can search for one more day then we'll head back tonight if we can't find them. We'll have to talk to the boss when we get within range of a cell tower. In the meantime, keep on the lookout for our guy and his girlfriend and watch for a place where we can get some gas."

They were getting impatient with searching the wild territory. They had already gotten lost a couple of times. It was only by chance that they managed to find the main road again. They wouldn't be able to search for another day without getting some gas. Up ahead they could see a small logging camp just off the road. A few camping trailers were setup for the workers. Dylan was happy to see some jerrycans sitting by one of the trailers. They pulled in and Dylan jumped out. The vehicles were all gone and camp was quiet. He tried knocking on one of the doors but there was no response. After looking around some more, Dylan grabbed three cans of gas and put them in the back of the truck.

They drove further down the road before dumping one can in their gas tank. It wouldn't be until later in the afternoon that they would turn onto Lost Axe Road and start heading toward Gabriel and Nicole's hiding spot.

* * *

Gabriel woke up first. He rubbed the sleep from his eyes and looked back at Nicole. She was sound asleep. He watched her for a few minutes. She looked so peaceful, so beautiful. He had never been in this kind of situation before. He'd had crushes like any other guy, and there had been some girls that liked him, but he had always been too nervous to get close to them. Now here was this incredible woman in his life. They had been thrust together by a series of unfortunate circumstances, yet those calamities were producing something good. He and Nicole were forging a bond that he hoped would continue to grow.

Nicole started to awaken and Gabriel stopped staring at her. She opened her eyes and tried to stretch. "Good morning," Gabriel said to her.

"Good morning," she replied with a yawn. "How'd you sleep?"

"Not bad for being in a truck. You?"

"About the same I guess."

Gabriel leaned his chair forward again and opened the door. There was still a chill in the morning air but the skies were clear so he hoped for a warm day. He went to the back to dig around for some food.

"Do you want nuts, fruit, or granola for breakfast?" he asked Nicole.

What she really wanted was pancakes but she settled for fruit and granola. Gabriel brought some back inside and they ate quietly.

"I think I'll go try some fishing while it's early," Gabriel finally stated.

"I should go with you for my lessons," she said with a smile.

They got the rods out and put them together. He grabbed the small tackle box and a fillet knife and they started down to the water. There was a small game trail they were able to follow. Nicole noticed how clean the air smelled. In Fort Frances the air often had a foul odour thanks to the mill, but out here there was nothing but water and forest to smell. She could see the appeal for outdoorsmen to camp out at a place like this. When they reached the water's edge, Gabriel started setting up the lines with lures.

"I don't think we'll be able to get any trout from shore here but we can go after pike. Have you ever seen one before?"

"No," she replied.

"This will be a treat for you then," he said with a grin. She wasn't sure why he was smiling so mischievously, but she didn't think much about it.

"Pike like these spoons," he explained. "To be honest, they will usually grab anything they see but I've found these especially tantalize them. Generally, if you think you'll be catching pike it's good to put a leader on the end of the line and attach your spoon to that. The spoon is heavy enough for casting so I won't stick any weights on. If we were out trolling for trout we would have to add weights to the line to get deep enough for them."

Nicole nodded and pretended she cared about the details as Gabriel showed her how to tie a knot in the line. Finally, the preparations were done and it was time to learn how to cast.

"Ok, here's how the reel works. Are you right-handed?"

"Yes," she said getting ready.

"Take the rod in your right hand like this." Nicole copied him as he showed her what to do. "Take your index finger and grab the line, then flip the top of the reel over. Once you let go with your finger the line will start going out so you have to let go at the right time. When you cast, if you let go too early, the spoon will end up falling behind you even though you fling the line forward. If you let go too late then the spoon will hit hard right in front of you. Make sense?"

"I think so. When do you let go?"

"As you bring the rod forward, like this," Gabriel made a beautiful long cast with his line and it gently hit the water.

"That seems easy enough," she told him with confidence. Gabriel just smiled and reeled in his line while she prepared to fling her lure into the water. She wound up for a big swing and brought the rod forward wildly, failing to let go of the line in time and the spoon swung back toward her, hitting the water's edge and splashing some up at her. She jumped and screamed a little. Gabriel turned away slightly so that she wouldn't see him suppressing a laugh.

Nicole glared at the rod. She set up the reel and tried again. This time she let go too soon and the spoon flew backward and landed in a tree so that when she pulled the rod forward she ended up releasing a bunch of line on the ground. "Stupid thing," she snorted.

"Don't get upset, it takes time to get a good rhythm down. Here, let me get your hook out of the tree."

Gabriel walked over and gently pulled on the line and moved the branch at the same time. The hook popped loose and he helped her reel the line back in.

"Keep trying it out. Maybe just try to be gentler swinging the rod. You don't have to whip it, ok?"

"Alright. So, you bring it back and let go of the line as you come forward, right?" she asked.

"Yes."

Nicole tried again with less force and this time she almost had it timed properly. The spoon flew forward a few feet and landed in the water.

"There you go," Gabriel praised her. "Just keep doing that and gradually you will get more distance out of it."

Nicole smiled proudly. She sometimes struggled with impatience but she was a quick learner. She kept practicing and gradually got smoother, gaining more distance. While she practiced, Gabriel got a bite. He set the hook and settled in for a fight.

"I've got one," he announced.

"It looks like a big one," she said looking at his rod bend.

"It's probably a fair size. Pike are good fighters, especially when the ice has just left. They're hungry and ready for a fight. Later in the year, they get a little more lethargic with the warmer water."

Gabriel kept playing with the fish for a couple minutes before bringing it in. "I like to let the fish play out before trying to grab them," he explained. "When I was a kid I just wanted to reel it in as fast as I could but I'd lose them when they got close because they'd jump and spit out the hook. My dad kept telling me to let them fight and slowly bring them closer so that when they come to the surface they don't jump around so much and they're easier to grab. Plus, it's more fun that way."

She was getting so excited watching him. He looked like he was having fun too. The fish finally appeared and Gabriel grabbed it to show Nicole.

"It's ugly!" she said with her nose wrinkled.

"Yes they are. See his teeth? They cut you pretty bad if you get your finger in there. Here, want to hold it?"

"Not really."

"Come on, this is part of fishing. Grab on."

He handed her the fish and she looked completely disgusted as the slime oozed around her fingers. Just as she thought she had a hold on it, the fish flailed and squirted up out of her hands and back into the water. Nicole just about fell in after it trying to grab the fish again before it swam away. In a flash, it was gone. Nicole stood there, stunned by what just happened. Gabriel started to roar with laughter. It was one of the funniest things he'd seen in a long time. She looked up at him a bit dazed, but then started to laugh too. She realized what a sight it must have been to watch her fumbling with a slimy fish. In that moment, as they laughed together, they forgot why they were out there in the first place. They weren't thinking about the people who had died and how close they had come to death themselves. They were just two friends having a good laugh over a silly fishing incident.

"I'm sorry," she said as she wiped joyful tears from her eyes. "I lost your fish."

"Don't worry about it. We can catch another one."

They continued casting together until Nicole had a fish latch onto her hook as soon as it hit the water. "I've got one," she squealed excitedly like a little girl.

Gabriel put his rod down and stepped over to help her. "Hang on tight because they'll pull pretty hard."

"Ok," she said nervously.

"Now pull back a little on the rod and reel in the slack. Keep the line tight or he'll spit the hook out. Just keep pulling back and then reeling in the slack. If he yanks and wants to run with the line then just keep it tight and let him go, then start reeling in when he slows down."

Nicole giggled and grinned in a way she hadn't in years. Gabriel had disarmed her tough, police shell and now she was completely herself with him. He continued to coach her over the next five minutes as she fought and reeled in her catch. It was a pike just a little smaller than the one Gabriel had caught. He reached down and grabbed the line close to the hook to lift the fish out of the water. Then he pulled it far enough away that they would not have to worry about losing it like the last one.

"It's a good size," he said to her. "We'll eat this one. Want to kiss it before it dies?"

Nicole just crinkled her nose and shook her head. He laughed and pulled out his knife. After putting it out of its misery he started to fillet the meat.

"Are all fish that slimy when they're fresh?" Nicole asked him.

"No. These ones are particularly bad. You can see why some people call them 'slimers'. Some guys buy special gloves that help you to keep a grip on them. It makes it a lot easier to pull out hooks and fillet them. See all the bones here?"

"Oh yeah. There's a lot of them."

"Some fish are pretty easy to fillet without getting any bones. With these things you have to learn a few tricks and practice to get all the bones out. Some people try to cook the meat with the skeleton still attached and then pull out the bones once the meat is softened up."

"Did your dad teach you all this stuff?"

"Mostly. I learned a few things from other people too."

"What did your dad do for work?"

"He was a forester. The mill hired him to help with regeneration of new forests. He loved being out here instead of cooped up in an office."

"What about your mom and brother?"

"Mom was a homemaker. She liked to cook and bake and do all that typical housewife stuff. Our house was near Reef Point in a private spot. My brother and I used to spend all summer fishing. We liked to play cards too. My dad was good at euchre and we played it often with him."

"That sounds nice. I wish I had grown up that way."

"Where are your parents?"

"They're still back in Toronto. Dad is a lawyer and my mom is a teacher. We got along fine but growing up in the city isn't the same as out here. It's always so busy. The traffic in Toronto was pretty ridiculous and sometimes Dad would come home very grumpy after a long day at work and a bad drive home. Hopefully my parents will retire soon. I have a sister who went into politics in Ottawa. To be honest, I don't really know what she's up to these days. I haven't talked to her much in the last few years. What about your brother?"

"He was still living at home when they had the accident. He was thinking of getting into computers. Alright, looks like this is done. Let's just wash up in the water and we can cook it for lunch."

The two made their way back to the truck, walking along the trail that took them through trees and a bunch of long grass. When they arrived at their temporary home, Gabriel set the fillets on a plate to get a fire ready. As he gathered up some kindling, he looked down at his arm and noticed a small wood tick crawling on his shirt. He pulled it off and started looking at his clothes. There were a few more on his pants. Ticks didn't bother him. He was used to picking them off. But Gabriel wasn't sure how Nicole would do if she found some.

"Hey, Nicole?"

"Yes," she answered.

"You might want to check yourself for ticks."

"Excuse me?"

"I think that we may have picked up a few in that long grass on the way back."

Nicole stared at him in disbelief. "Ticks...on me..."

Gabriel walked over and showed her one of the ones that had been on him. He was a little worried when she started hyperventilating and shaking her hands.

"It's ok," he tried to reassure her. "If they're on you just pick them off."

"What if they're attached? What do I do? Can't you die if their head gets in your skin?"

"Just breathe deep breaths. Don't panic. You're not going to die."

"Please just get them off me!"

"Ok. I will."

Gabriel started looking at her clothes for any ticks. He realized as he did it that this was probably the type of thing most guys would love to do. Even though he was still quite nervous with her, the man in him couldn't help but smile a little. Carefully he checked her clothes, taking a couple ticks off. Stepping away, he declared her clothes clean.

"You should check underneath your clothes," he advised. "I'll go on the other side of the truck to check myself."

"Great!" she muttered. "What do I do if I find one?"

"Just call and I'll tell you."

Gabriel walked around and started stripping down. He found one crawling along his skin but that was it. Looking his clothes over carefully again he started getting dressed.

"I found one," she called.

"Is it attached?" he wanted to know.

"No, it's moving."

"Then just grab it and throw it off." He smiled and rolled his eyes. She was obviously still a bit of a city girl but she was getting an education.

"I think one is attached. It isn't moving."

"What you need to do is grab it as close to the your skin as you can and gently pull it off, taking a piece of skin with it."

"What? Are you messing with me?"

"No, just do what I said."

"I don't know…"

"Do you want me to…?"

"Not really. But I can't get a good hold on it and I'm afraid I won't do it right."

There was an awkward silence. Gabriel didn't know what else to tell her and she didn't really want him coming over. Finally she asked, "What happens if I don't pull it off properly?"

"Don't think about that. Just focus on getting it off."

That wasn't what she wanted to hear. She closed her eyes, folded her arms and reluctantly made a decision. "Please come here and get it off."

Gabriel had finished getting dressed so he walked back around and stopped suddenly. There was this gorgeous woman standing with her back to him…with nothing on.

"Maybe you should put some clothes back on," he said.

"Just look at my butt."

He looked at it. It was hard not to. He could see the problem. The tick was attached to her right cheek. Moving forward he knelt down and reached for it.

"The tick had better be the only thing you grab," she cautioned.

He paused and looked up at her. Her head was turned and her eyes were piercing him. Carefully, he gripped onto it and yanked it off with ease. It was barely attached. He turned away and cleared his throat.

"All better now," he said.

She scurried to get her clothes back on and Gabriel went back to the fire situation. He got a fire lit and started cooking the fish using a small pan that he had thrown into the emergency kit. When Nicole settled down from the tick ordeal she came over to the fire.

"Thank you for your help," she said quietly.

"You're welcome."

"I'm sorry I got so riled up over that. I'm a little embarrassed."

"Don't worry about it. I guess it's easy to get worked up over something you've never dealt with before."

"Are there always ticks like that here?"

"No. Actually I haven't seen them this far north before."

Nicole calmed down and sat on a stump by the fire. Looking at Gabriel again she was thankful that he was a gentleman. He didn't make any comments or try anything while she was totally exposed. She still felt a bit foolish over the whole thing. Gabriel decided to change the subject for her.

"So, anyway, pike actually has tasty meat if you eat it fresh from cold water. Once it gets hot out it isn't very good but this one should be nice to eat. Some people only want to eat walleye but I don't mind having a little pike in the springtime."

"You sure seem to know your fish."

"Just a few," he stated modestly.

"You know, Gabriel, you didn't tell me what you do for work?"

"That's because I don't have a job."

"You never had one?"

"Sure I did. When I was done school I wanted to learn a trade so I moved out west and spent a few years learning carpentry and also worked with a mason for a while to learn how to do stone and bricks."

"Did you build your house?"

"Most of it. I had someone pour the foundation and put up the frame because I didn't want to do that myself. But I did all the stone and everything inside except for the drywall mud and tape. I hate doing that so I hired that out too."

"That's pretty impressive. What happened with your job?"

"When the accident happened I came home to care for the estates. My parents had socked away quite a bit of money selling off property that they owned on the lakefront. They inherited the land and decided to sell because they weren't using it and it was in high demand. Between inheriting that money and the life insurance they had, I was setup pretty well. I decided to forget about the hustle and bustle of working life. I bought that property, built the house and set things up so that I shouldn't have to work again."

"Wow. That's everybody's dream!"

"I guess it is. I enjoy it."

"Don't you find it boring sometimes?"

"Not usually. There's lots to do around the house and I go fishing as much as I can. The winter can be dull so I read a fair bit and take trips to warmer locations. Sometimes it is lonely being by myself though."

"So why do live that far away from everything?"

"I don't know. I guess I just like the peaceful surroundings more than having a bunch of neighbors around. I do have friends to hang out with sometimes, like John…" Gabriel trailed off after he mentioned his friend's name. Memories of their activities together starting coming back to mind. He looked at Nicole and she could see that his eyes were starting to get glossy with tears. "I'm going to miss him a little," he said. "It seems like all the people I've known keep dying off."

Gabriel managed to stop himself from crying and asked Nicole, "Were you and Frank close?"

"We were good friends. If you're referring to romance, we were never involved. He was married with a couple of children. But he was a good partner.

It's still hard to believe he's gone…" Now it was Nicole's turn to cry, except she couldn't fight the tears back. She started crying uncontrollably and Gabriel felt terrible for bringing up Frank. He stepped over and held her while she cried.

"I just feel so sorry for his family," she sobbed. "I think a lot of people will miss him."

After a few minutes she got the tears out of her system. She felt better. It had been buried inside and felt good to release some of the emotions. She thanked Gabriel and went to find a tissue in the truck. When she got back the fish was ready to eat.

"I think there might be some salt and pepper in the cab left over from the drive-thru," he told her. Walking over he found some in the glove box. "Here we are. Would you like a little seasoning with your fish?"

"Sure," she said. "Hey, this is pretty good. I'm surprised with how little ingredients we had to cook it. I like it."

"It probably helps that we haven't been eating very well lately," Gabriel said with a smile.

"Do you mind if I ask you something else?" she said while they ate.

"Go ahead."

"Have you ever been married?"

He looked a little surprised and uncomfortable with the question. "No," was his reply.

"Why not?"

"I guess the opportunity never really presented itself. I was never very popular."

"I find that hard to believe."

"It's true. I was the quiet one in school."

"What about after school?"

"I don't know. I just always find it hard to converse with strangers. I don't know what to talk about. Honestly, how many women want to go on a date with a guy that can only talk about fishing?"

"I see your point. But if you never try then how can you improve?"

"I suppose that's true. You wouldn't find it hard to spend time with someone who is quiet a lot?"

"I don't know…you have other things that you excel at right? I think the right woman would look past a lack of conversation skills and see the gems under the surface."

Gabriel looked down at the ground, digesting what she had just said. She was right. He had given up on women because he found it hard to get to know people but he needed to seek ways to improve and give people a chance. He needed to think about this some more.

"What about you? Were you ever married?"

"No. I had a serious relationship once but it turned out I wasn't the only one he was interested in so I called it off. Lately I've kept myself busy with work and left it at that."

The conversation hit a stand-still at that point. Neither one knew what to say. The silence was broken by the sound of a vehicle approaching. Both of them were thinking the same thing. Was it those guys looking for them? Gabriel kicked out the fire.

"Should we go get a look at them?" he asked.

"Yes, we should. Can we get back to the road in time?"

"We'll have to run."

They started jogging back down the trail they had driven in on. The truck was slowly moving along the road but they heard it reach the dead end just as they were running within view. They hid behind some bushes and listened. Someone got out of the truck and they could hear him yell, "Looks like whoever came back here just turned around and headed out again." The door slammed shut as he got back in and the truck turned around. As it came back up over the hill where Gabriel had turned off, they caught a glimpse of the driver. It was the one who had been after them.

They held their breath as Dylan paused at the top of the hill to look around. It was only a moment then he carried on, going back faster than he had come. If Dylan had been more careful, they might have noticed where the vehicle had turned off, but they missed it and were going to make their way out.

"I think we're ok," Nicole stated. "Let's go back."

*   *   *

After turning around and driving back the way they came, Dylan looked down at the gas gauge. They had already dumped all the gas they stole into the truck and it looked like they would only have enough left to make it home.

"There's too many roads to search up here," he told the others. "Let's just go home and call the boss."

They agreed and the group started making the long drive back to Fort Frances. It had been a miserable assignment to take out Gabriel and they had failed. Their boss would not be happy with them.

CHAPTER 9

Gabriel was mentally debating whether or not they should try to go home. "Do you think those guys will be hanging around?" he asked Nicole.

"I don't know. If they keep searching then they won't come back here but I'm sure they won't stay around for very long. They will have to go home eventually and come up with another plan."

"I was wondering if it would be best to stay put for now or if we should try something?"

"What did you have in mind?"

"Back near the entrance to Lost Axe Road there is a cabin maintained by the mill in town. Their employees use it when they are supervising tree planting and spraying herbicide on trees. They have a phone there as well as full cooking facilities. If we could get in then we could make a call for help and have a bed to sleep in."

Nicole thought about it and said, "That might be a good idea. Why don't we wait here a little longer and head out before dark."

They cleaned up camp and packed the truck again. After they felt it was safe to go they slowly drove back toward the cabin. Both of them kept their eyes peeled for a possible run-in with their foes, but they were long gone. When Gabriel came to the junction of Cedar Narrows and Lost Axe he turned left to go south. A short distance down the road there was a sign pointing to Rabbit Lake on the right side. Turning right, he started down the winding driveway to the cabin.

Coming up to the peak of a hill, the cabin appeared near the bottom of the slope. Past the cabin the hill continued steeply down about a hundred meters to the water's edge. The trees opened up to reveal the lake, with a dock in the shape of an L. The cabin was nothing fancy but the view was beautiful. As they coasted down the hill Nicole saw two buildings situated up and to the side of the cabin. One looked like a small garage and the other appeared to have a chimney poking through the roof.

Gabriel pulled up beside the cabin and hopped out. He knocked loudly on the door but there was no answer. He tried the handle and the door swung open. "Looks like someone forgot to lock the door," he announced.

"Maybe they leave it open," Nicole suggested.

"That could be. There definitely isn't anyone around." Pointing up at the building with the small chimney he said, "I think there is a generator up there. I'll go see if I can get it started."

Nicole walked inside and looked around. From the door there was a small hallway leading straight ahead with a closet to the left. As she exited the hallway it opened up to a dining room with a large window providing a view of the lake. To her immediate left was a bathroom with a shower. To the left of the dining room was a full kitchen tucked in the corner. The fridge and stove ran on gas. She remembered that just outside the cabin was a large propane tank which obviously ran these appliances.

Turning right she was looking down the length of the building. It had the open concept for the rooms except for the bedrooms which were all located to the right side behind the wall. In the dining room was an electric stove for heat. Beyond was the living room with two couches and a television. It also had a large window revealing the water below. There was another exit on the far end of the living room with a deck outside. The bedrooms totalled three. One of them had a double bed and the other two each had a single bed and two bunks stacked against the one wall.

Nicole turned quickly when she heard the sound of an engine firing up loudly. Then the lights started to flicker on and she realized that Gabriel had started the generator. Walking into the kitchen she started to dig through the cupboards.

When Gabriel came back inside she told him, "Looks like there is some canned food here we could eat. They probably don't leave perishable food lying around. Should we start cooking up some supper?"

"Sure. How about if I do that while you make a phone call?"

"Sounds good. I'll call the station."

Nicole went to the phone and dialled Jack Rudiger's office. "Rudiger here," was the gruff answer.

"Hi, it's Nicole."

"Edouard?" Jack exclaimed.

"Yes, sir."

Jack's voice went quiet as though he was afraid someone might hear him. "Where are you?"

"I'm with Gabriel in a cabin in the middle of nowhere."

"What on earth happened to you?"

"We were watching Gabriel's place when we were attacked. A group of guys chased us and we had to hide out up here. We just got to this cabin so we could call for help."

"Ok, I'll get the whole story when we pick you up. I want the two of you to stay there right now. I will send someone for you in the morning. Where exactly is your location?"

Nicole gave him detailed directions and hung up the phone. It felt like a humongous weight had been lifted off her. There was a light at the end of the tunnel. All they had to do now was wait patiently and everything would be fine. Looking up she could see Gabriel had supper well under way.

"Well, it sounds like we're in the clear," she told him.

"That's good news. What's the plan?"

"We'll wait here for a pickup and then go after those guys with the force backing us up."

"So we have some time to waste then?"

"Yes we do. What do you want to do?"

"There might be some cards or board games around. We could play something if you want. They might have a few movies here too."

"I'll see what's here."

Nicole started digging through the shelves around the TV and found some movies, but nothing she wanted to watch. Next to the videos there were a few decks of cards and a cribbage game.

"I found some cards. None of the movies are worth watching."

"Ok," replied Gabriel. "What games do you know?"

"Just a few that two people can play. Let me see…there's 'go fish' and 'war.' We could play 'cribbage.'"

"It's been a long time since I played 'crib.' I suppose I could try that one. Supper should be ready in a minute here."

The two ate some canned soup and then started shuffling the deck. Gabriel spent at least ten minutes trying to get the rules straight. He lost the first couple rounds, which was ok because Nicole clearly enjoyed winning. The third time was definitely the charm, as Gabriel almost skunked her. Time passed by speedily as they spent the evening laughing and playing around.

Unknown to Gabriel and Nicole, outside two men dressed in dark clothes moved quickly through the night air. One of them stopped at the top of the hill looking down at the cabin. He was to stay there and keep watch. The other man, Dylan, quietly moved toward the cabin. He stopped briefly to look up at the night sky. The northern lights were dancing vibrantly. He caught himself and focused on the task at hand.

Walking up onto the deck he carefully looked through the window to see Gabriel and Nicole seated at the table. He leaned back and stepped off the deck. An evil grin formed across his lips as he placed an explosive device under the large propane tank. He couldn't have asked for a better setup to destroy the place and make it look like an accident. After setting the bomb he returned to his partner at the top of the hill. His partner was staring at the lights in the sky until he realized the other thug was back.

"Are we ready to go?" the one on the hill whispered.

"Yes, it's in place."

They both looked at the cabin again before one of them pressed the detonation button on a wireless remote. When the propane tank exploded it sent a deafening blast past them. It completely decimated the cabin and pieces of the building were scattered all over the forest and into the lake. What didn't get blasted apart was quickly burned up as a fire roared over the place. It didn't take long for the heat to spark an explosion in Gabriel's truck and it leaped straight up in the air when the fuel ignited. Pieces of metal and wood were widely dispersed, starting some of the bush on fire. The size of the blast even impressed the two murderers, and they congratulated each other on a successful mission.

The two men returned to their vehicle which was parked just at the edge of the entrance to the driveway. Their consciences were not bothered at all by what they had just done. They were hardened criminals who relished the opportunity to return the favour to the two people who killed their comrades. They were going home now, extremely satisfied.

CHAPTER 10

The fire from the cabin continued to burn for an hour or so before it died down. The fire in the vegetation did not spread very far thanks to the wet spring. Down by the dock, some of the debris started to move as Gabriel stood up. His head was spinning a little and his body ached from being struck by pieces of the building. He looked around to get his bearings. The last thing he remembered was walking down the slope to the lake. He and Nicole had slipped out the back door unobserved in order to watch the northern lights. Panic hit him as he started searching for Nicole. He called her name and frantically pulled debris away from the area to find her.

After calling her name several times, Gabriel heard a soft moan nearby. He moved toward the sound and lifted some shingles to reveal Nicole's body. He knelt beside her and spoke. "Nicole! Can you hear me?"

"Yes," she whispered and coughed. "What happened?"

"I don't know. Are you ok?"

"I think so. My arm hurts, though."

Gabriel looked at it. It was badly bruised and scraped a little but didn't look broken. She was able to move it. He got her to sit up and then gradually to stand. Both of them were banged up but otherwise fine. They slowly walked up the hill to where the cabin used to be.

"It looks like there was an explosion," Nicole said. "Wasn't there a propane tank here?"

"Yes, there was. There might have been a leak. But what would have caused the ignition?"

Nicole knelt down where the tank had been and looked closely but it was too dark to see much. "Do you have a flashlight?" she asked Gabriel.

"There should still be one in the truck." He started walking to where he parked only to discover the remains of what used to be his truck. Gabriel's heart sank. Not only had they almost been killed, a few times, but now they were stuck without a way out of the bush. Dejected, he went back to Nicole and pointed toward the charred body of the truck.

"Oh no. What do we do now?" she said aloud. "I guess we will need to find some cover for the night and look at this mess in the morning. Then we have to find a way out of here. What do you think?"

"We could probably use the shed over there for the night. It looks to be intact."

The two shuffled over to the shed and went inside. It was pitch black so they felt around and discovered a pile of life vests that they put on the floor for cushions. Gabriel opened a window for fresh air and closed the door. Both of them lay on the floor going over what they remembered. While they wanted to think it was an accident from a leak in the propane tank, they couldn't fight the nagging feeling that someone had tried to kill them again.

Gabriel finally asked, "Do you think that someone could have set off the explosion?"

"Honestly, I have a bad feeling that is the case. I should be able to find the source of the explosion when the sun comes up. What bothers me most is not that someone may have tried to kill us. What bothers me is that if someone did try to kill us then how did they know where we were? Only one person knew, Jack Rudiger, my boss. If he is somehow involved in this mess then I don't know how we are going to get out of this and clean everything up."

Gabriel was beginning to feel hopelessly lost. He had moved to Robson Lake to seek the peace and quiet that nature could offer him. Now his life would be forever altered by the chaos that had entered it. Would he get past this? How could he? Why were these criminals so desperate to get rid of him and everyone that gets near that island? As he lay there trying to get to sleep his thoughts turned back to his friend, John. Gabriel felt that his initial suspicions about John's death had some basis. What if John had seen something he shouldn't have? Is that why he died? Or was it actually an accident?

Gabriel couldn't stop the questions circling in his mind. There seemed to be no answers in sight at this point. Nicole was not faring much better. Endless arrays of questions were floating in her head as well. Was the explosion an accident? If not, how did Jack get pulled into all of this? What other explanation could there be? Where could she and Gabriel turn for help now? How were they going to solve this mystery and get their lives back? Both of them spent an hour or two wrestling with these thoughts before they finally succumbed to the fatigue their bodies felt and fell asleep.

*   *   *

The birds were chirping happily in the morning when Gabriel and Nicole awoke. For a moment Gabriel hoped everything from the night before was nothing more than a bad dream. Looking around at the shed they had slept in told him that it was no dream. He was still stuck in the most miserable experience of his life. He stood up and rubbed his aching back. He wasn't sure if it hurt from the blast or from sleeping on the ground. Nicole opened the door and they both stepped outside. It was a beautiful day and the sun was blinding them at first. They stared at what was left of the cabin. It was just a tangled mess of scorched wood and wire. The pickup was just a blackened shell of a vehicle.

Nicole walked down to where the propane tank had been to investigate and Gabriel kicked at what remained from his truck. He hollered at Nicole, "I was thinking last night that we might be able to catch a ride out with a truck driver."

"That is probably our only option isn't it?"

"I would say so."

"Gabriel, come look at this. I found something."

He started to run but quickly realized that was a bad idea. He was still too sore for that. Walking to Nicole he looked down where she was pointing. "See the marks here?" she asked. "Those must have been made by a small explosive that started the fire. Once it went off it caused the tank to blow and the cabin went with it. I think the heat probably ignited your truck. They could have placed an explosive on it too but I doubt it. They came here for us and likely made sure we were inside when they placed it."

"How come they didn't set it off in time?" he asked her.

"They would have had to get out of harm's way. I bet they were up the hill when it went off. They may have used a timer or a remote to detonate it. I guess we picked a good time to check out the northern lights last night. They must not have seen us leave and by the time of the blast we were almost at the lake. That's why we only have cuts and bruises."

"So, what do we do now? It sounds like your boss is involved, right?"

"Yes it does. I have a friend that might be able to help. He lives in Dryden. He is also an officer. We went through training together. I trust him. Right now I don't trust anyone at the detachment in the Fort. Jack might have others on his side there. I think we should try to catch a ride to Dryden and make plans on what to do next when we get there."

"I guess I should clean up in the lake a little and we can start hitch-hiking." Gabriel went to the dock and scooped up some water to wash his face. There was some dried blood and dust that came off. The water was still quite cold and putting it on his face gave him a burst of exhilaration. Nicole appeared at his side and washed her face as well. Both of them looked like they had been in a scrap with someone. Their clothes were torn, their hair was scraggly and their skin was scabby. All they could do was laugh. It was either that or cry and neither one was willing to lose their endurance yet.

The pair started trekking up the driveway to the main road. They had no idea how they would get out of the bush but they were certain of one thing: they would find out who was responsible for all of this and make them pay.

"We do have one thing in our favour at this point," Nicole told Gabriel.

"Oh? What's that?"

"We now have the element of surprise. They think we're both dead. Hopefully that false sense of security will allow us to catch them red-handed."

"Yes, that would be a nice feeling."

Though Gabriel was a quiet man who did not wish ill on anyone, he had been pushed too far. While he would normally walk away if confronted, his loathing for the people threatening him and Nicole was so strong now that there was no way he would just run away. They needed to experience what it was like to be the prey for once.

After walking down Cedar Narrows Road for a couple of hours they could hear the rumbling of a pulp truck coming toward them from the North. Gabriel motioned for Nicole to get off the road and he got ready to hail the driver. The truck popped up over the hill behind them and Gabriel waved his arms to get his attention. It took the driver some time to stop and Gabriel and Nicole ran up to the passenger door.

"We can't tell him the truth," Nicole whispered to Gabriel before he climbed up.

"Is there something wrong?" the driver asked.

"Yes," Gabriel told him. "My friend and I are stranded. We had car trouble and need to get some help."

"I have some tools you could use," the driver said smiling.

"No, um, I'm afraid it is a little more extensive than that. We need a ride out and I'll have to come back later to get it."

"I see. Well, you can hop in if you want with your friend and I'll take you as far as I can."

"Thank you so much."

The driver was a middle-aged man with a warm, honest face. He had creases in his forehead and crow's feet at the side of his eyes when he smiled. They climbed into the cab but there was only one extra seat. Gabriel looked back at Nicole and nervously tried to think of how to arrange things. He didn't want to sit on her and he couldn't see where else he could sit.

"I'm afraid she'll have to sit on your lap," the driver said with a chuckle. "Such a terrible predicament," he stated sarcastically and laughed. "Come on, we have to get going."

Gabriel sat down and Nicole sat on his lap, then closed the door. Gabriel never had anything in his lap before other than maybe a dog or cat. He couldn't help feeling a bit awkward but, then again, after pulling a tick from her cheek, having her sit on him really wasn't that big of a deal.

"So, you said that you are friends. I take it you two aren't married?"

"No, we aren't," Gabriel said quickly.

"Uh huh. So, what's wrong then? You afraid of commitment?" he asked Gabriel.

"No," he retorted defensively. "Why do you think we're together anyway?"

"Oh, come on. The two of you alone together out here?"

"Gabriel here is just a little shy," Nicole said and smiled at him. "We're . . . close friends."

"I see. Oh, I'm sorry I didn't introduce myself. My name is Bob. So, you're Gabriel and what's your name ma'am?"

"Nicole."

"It's nice to meet you both. I'm sorry it's under these circumstances. Where are you from?"

"Dryden," Nicole replied quickly.

"Well, I can take you part way but I'm actually headed to Fort Frances with this load. If you want I can check with a friend to see if he could take you the rest of the way. He's fishing near Highway 502 and will be headed up to Dryden when he's done."

"That would be great," Nicole told him.

They continued to chat as they watched the scenery race past them. Nicole didn't notice a sharp curve coming up and when they steered into it she lost her balance and fell against Gabriel. His strong arms came up quickly to catch her. They looked into each other's eyes and stayed locked like that for a moment. Nicole felt safe being held in his arms. Gabriel didn't want to let go. Nicole slowly looked away, as did Gabriel. However, he did not let go of her. He kept her close to him, as though he was afraid that if he let go she would disappear from his life. Nicole stayed where she was, happy to stay poised like that eternally.

Bob looked at the two and smiled. He could sense this was new love. They had the look of a couple that was still so enamoured with each other that the world around stopped moving. Bob thought back to the time when he and his wife were like that. They were still very much in love but sometimes he wished he could go back to when they had first met and experience the euphoria of dating all over again.

Gabriel clung to Nicole for the rest of the journey on Cedar Narrows Road. It wasn't long before they approached the spot where the pulp truck had slammed into one of their pursuers. Bob slowed right down as he got closer.

"It's a shame what happened here a few days ago," Bob said.

Gabriel decided to play dumb. "Was there an accident?" he asked.

"Yes, a bad one. One of my friends was on his way out hauling a load and he slammed into a passenger vehicle. I guess the folks inside died instantly. He squished them into the rock over there," he said pointing. "His truck flipped and left a pretty bad mess. It took them a while to clean everything up."

"Did he die too?"

"No, he lived. He's in the hospital with bad injuries and it sounds like he'll pull through. I think he'll have a long recovery though."

"I'm sorry," Gabriel told him.

"It's not your fault."

Gabriel almost said that it actually was his fault but he just turned and looked out the window. Flashbacks of the accident came into his mind. He continued holding Nicole but his head was no longer swimming with happy emotions. He was reminded of the mess they both found themselves in and he lost all feelings of happiness as he started contemplating their demise again.

When they came within a few kilometers of the highway, Bob made a call on the radio to his friend. The man was just getting ready to leave and said that he would be able to take Gabriel and Nicole with him. They met at the highway and changed vehicles. They thanked Bob for his help and climbed into the back of an SUV. Inside, Bob's friend introduced himself.

"My name is Brent," he told them and shook their hand.

A woman in the front seat smiled and said, "I'm his wife, Doreen." She was a little hard to understand with her accent. It sounded to them like she had marbles in her mouth when she spoke. As they started driving, Doreen couldn't seem to stop talking and Gabriel and Nicole had no idea what she was talking about. The husband would laugh like she had told a joke so they both decided to laugh along like they knew what was happening. Doreen just kept flapping her gums but they still had no idea what was wrong with her. When they did understand the words she said it seemed like she bounced in and out of topics every few seconds.

Gabriel looked at Nicole with confusion written on his face and got the same look back at him. What was wrong with this woman? Was her husband crazy too? Both of them were the oddest human beings either Gabriel or Nicole had met. Bob had seemed so normal. How could he have friends like this? Finally Gabriel just stared out the window and replied, "Oh yeah...uh huh," periodically. He decided that the marbles in Doreen's mouth must have come from her mind. That explained everything.

It was an extremely long trip to Dryden. It seemed like it would never end when the town finally came into sight. They asked to be dropped off at a restaurant not far from the home of Nicole's friend. When the car stopped, Gabriel jumped out like it was on fire and headed for the restaurant. He yelled 'thank you' over his shoulder.

Gabriel stood at the restaurant door and put on a fake smile while he waited to make sure the world's strangest couple left. Nicole laughed at Gabriel's face. He looked completely bewildered.

"What?" he cried. "They creep me out, ok?" Nicole kept laughing and walked inside. Gabriel started to laugh too. His life had never had so many strange events as the last few days. They sat in a booth and ordered two drinks and some food. They were starving and wanted to eat before they found Nicole's friend.

After their meal they took a walk. The house was a few blocks away. Nicole kept an eye on the surroundings as they walked up to the door and rang the bell. The door swung open, revealing a short but stocky man with red hair.

"Nicole! How nice to see you. Come on in. Who's your friend?"

"This is Gabriel. Gabriel, meet Justin."

The two men shook hands and they went inside. The house was small but nicely furnished. They sat in the living room.

"What brings you here?" Justin inquired.

"I'm afraid it's not just to say hello," Nicole told him. "We're in trouble."

Justin's face became serious and he lowered his gaze. "What kind of trouble?"

Nicole and Gabriel proceeded to explain the whole story to Justin. His eyes widened in shock when they told him of the attempts on their lives. At the end of the story he sat quietly shaking his head.

"This sounds like something that happens in the movies. What do you think they are trying to protect?"

"It can't just be those goons we arrested. There has to be something big that they are hiding on that island."

"You didn't see anything?"

"Nothing. Either they moved it or it is well hidden."

"If the detachment is corrupt then maybe it would be wise to keep this to ourselves for the time being just in case there are others involved up here. I can probably take some time to help figure out what is going on. Why don't you stay here for now with me and I will get some things in order. Then we can go down together and figure out the mystery."

Justin told them where everything was and left to make some arrangements. Gabriel and Nicole put some blankets on the couch and floor. There was only one bedroom so they would have to sleep in the living room that night.

"This beats the shed we slept in last night," Gabriel said. "You can have the couch and I'll take the floor."

"I just hope I sleep a little better tonight. Do you want a drink? I know Justin always has some scotch around."

"I'd love one."

They watched TV for the evening and sipped on the scotch until Justin came back. He walked inside with a couple of duffel bags full of equipment for surveillance and weapons.

"I see you made yourself comfortable," he said with a grin. "I think we'll have everything we need. We can head out tomorrow morning in my unmarked police cruiser. I booked a few days off."

"Thank you, Justin," Nicole said. "I'm sorry to drag you into this."

"No worries. I'm happy to help you both. Let's get some rest."

They turned off the TV and got ready for bed. Gabriel finally felt relaxed after having a couple drinks and lying down. He said good night to Nicole and closed his eyes. In less than a minute he was asleep and he was going to need a good night's rest to face what was coming to him.

CHAPTER 11

T he water remained calm as a young man named Jason Whitehead paddled his canoe along the shoreline of Rainy Lake. He was a young man who loved the beauty of nature. Jason was paddling his way to a fishing hole his grandfather used to take him to. He had not been there for a number of years and decided to try it out again. Along the way he encountered a boat coming toward him. He turned the canoe to face the wake and waved as they passed. The men in the boat just looked away and kept driving.

"Jerks," Jason muttered. Most locals would at least wave. "They must be tourists that came to rob the fish supply," he thought to himself. He kept paddling and looked into the bay that they had come out of. There was a place at shore where they likely had stopped. Another boat was sitting there. He could tell that someone had pulled in there a number of times and packed a trail going into the forest. It seemed strange for it to be so well used. After all, this was Reserve land owned by his tribe. Jason was a member of the First Nations. As far as he knew, no one had anything all the way out here and he would have heard if someone built a house.

Unable to resist his own curiosity, Jason looked back to make sure the boat was out of view and paddled into the next bay. He pulled ashore and cut across to the trail. Following it into the trees, the trail wound through the rough terrain for at least a kilometer before a clearing appeared. He could hear some noise coming from the clearing so he stayed hidden in the trees. Carefully looking into the clearing, he noticed some men digging and sifting through the earth while a woman looked on and hollered orders to them. It looked like they had some equipment there to help them. Jason couldn't get close enough to figure out what was going on. They were obviously searching for something but what was it?

Jason thought about getting closer but he knew they would spot him right away without any cover. He decided to go back to the lake and figure out what was happening another way. Slipping away silently, he got back into his canoe and did some fishing before heading back home. While he fished he pondered the possibilities of what those men were digging for. None of them appeared to be First Nations. Why would they be on Reserve land? He would ask the chief when he returned home.

*   *   *

Gabriel, Nicole and Justin got up early and drove to Gabriel's house. Near the driveway they pulled over and parked the car. They had decided to hike in close to the house without driving in, just in case someone was watching the place. They got out and grabbed what gear they needed. Once ready, Gabriel led them into the trees and headed down a trail toward the lake. He slowed down as they approached the shoreline and pointed in the direction of the house.

"The water's edge is just ahead and the house is directly across," he told the two police officers.

"Why don't you stay here and we'll check it out," Nicole told him.

Nicole and Justin quietly walked to a good vantage point and pulled out their binoculars. Nicole scanned the yard and the house, but saw no sign of any intruders. Nick, the dog, was nowhere in sight either.

"Do you see anything," she asked Justin.

"No, it looks quiet. Do you think they would have surveillance setup nearby?"

"It's possible, but I would think that if someone was around they would be in the house. At this point they think both Gabriel and I are dead. They may not even be watching the place anymore."

"Why don't we head in to the house slowly and check it out?"

"Ok. I'll get Gabriel and he should be able to guide us along where no one can see us."

Gabriel led them down another trail he was familiar with. It would take them right up to the driveway without being seen. The whole way they kept a close eye on their surroundings but everything looked normal. Once they reached the driveway the officers took the lead with guns drawn and Gabriel followed closely. He looked around wild-eyed, imagining some crazy thug popping out of the bushes and mowing them down with an automatic weapon.

His heart was pounding in his chest and he could hear it in his ears as they came up beside the house. Nicole signalled silently that she would go around the back door and Justin took the front. They told Gabriel to stay outside and he was happy to oblige.

After checking the doors over carefully both officers lunged inside. There was nothing on the first floor, so they went upstairs and checked the bedrooms. The house was completely empty. Nicole put her sidearm away and shook her head.

"What's wrong?" inquired Justin.

"Something isn't right." She walked back to the stairs and looked out over the living room. "Frank's body is gone." Nicole ran down the stairs to where his body had been when they escaped. "There isn't any sign of blood. They must have cleaned up the scene. Look at the window."

"It looks fine to me," said Justin.

"Exactly! When we left it had shattered from the bullets coming through. When I look around now I can't spot a single sign that there was a murder here. Everything is in its place. Why would they clean it all up like this?"

"I don't know. I can see why they would get rid of the body but I don't understand why they would fix the window and everything else that got wrecked."

"It doesn't make sense."

Nicole walked to the window and looked out at the lake. She felt like she was trapped in a labyrinth. Everything they had gone through to this point was so confusing. Why were they attacked and chased? Why would everything at Gabriel's house be cleaned up so quickly, especially if they thought Gabriel and Nicole were dead?

Justin went outside and told Gabriel it was clear to come in. He noticed the changes right away.

"Did someone clean up in here? Wasn't there glass all over the place when we left?" he asked Nicole.

"Yes. I don't know what's going on," she replied.

Gabriel went upstairs and looked for his valuables. Everything was in place. He went back down and announced that nothing was missing. There was one thing gone though: Nick. He wondered what happened to his dog.

"I'm going to check the garage for Nick," Gabriel told them.

"I'll go with you," Nicole said.

The two walked outside cautiously and walked to the garage. Nicole opened the door and scanned the area before she let Gabriel go inside. He looked around and called for Nick but there was no response.

"I'm sorry Gabriel," Nicole said softly.

"It's ok. He may have run away. I guess we can look for him when this is all over with. What do we do now?"

"Now, we have to do some police work. We will have to watch Jack and see if he can lead us to the answers we're looking for. In the meantime, I don't think we should stick around here. We'll have to find a place to stay in town. Come on, let's get Justin and go back to the car."

Gabriel followed Nicole to the door then turned around and looked at the spot where his pickup used to be parked. He sighed deeply. It was a good truck, Nick was a good dog, and this had been a good home until John's dead body washed up. He prayed that one day he would get all those things back.

Turning around, Gabriel closed the door and followed Nicole and Justin back out to the car. They hopped in and continued their drive to Fort Frances.

CHAPTER 12

Jason Whitehead walked into the home of Ronald Crow. Ronald was a tall kind-looking man in his early fifties. His hair was still raven black but his face showed signs of age with some heavy wrinkles. His fingers were permanently stained thanks to the cigarette habit he'd had as long as Jason knew him.

"Hi Chief," Jason said respectfully.

"Hello Jason. How are you today?"

"Ok. I have a question for you."

"Well, what is it?" Ronald asked.

"I was out fishing by Longhorn Point and noticed some activity at the beach. I pulled into the next bay and went back to see what was going on. The trail took me inland about a kilometer where it opened up to a clearing and I saw some white men digging around the area with equipment. I thought it was suspicious because that's our land. Do you know of anything taking place there?"

"No I don't, especially not with white people doing it. It seems strange to me. No one ever goes out there. Can you show me where it is?"

"Sure."

The two men casually made their way down to the water where Jason's canoe was still sitting. No one on the Reserve seemed to move quickly, ever. Time meant little to them. Everything was done according to a different pace as soon as you entered the community. Their slow saunter to the water set the pace for their paddling as well. Slowly they worked their way out of the cove on which the Reserve was situated.

Once out in the open lake Jason steered the canoe in the direction of Longhorn Point. By the time they got there the sun was starting to make its descent on the horizon. Bright flashes of pink began soaring across the sky. They pulled into the same spot Jason had parked before and stepped onto shore. Jason led the way onto the main trail and Ronald followed behind. As they approached the clearing, the hum of a generator could be heard along with some excited speech.

It was getting dark now and they easily slipped behind cover to see what was going on. Some bright floodlights hooked up to the generator illuminated the area. Half a dozen men could be seen working around what appeared to be a small pit. Then the roar of a diesel engine could be heard as a skid-steer zipped up out of the pit. It stopped beside the men and a scruffy looking man with a permanent scowl on his face jumped out. He muttered something and one of the others quickly jumped inside the machine then disappeared into the pit. Before long the skid-steer could no longer be heard.

"What could they possibly be doing?" Jason whispered to Ron.

"I have no idea. There is nothing out here for them to dig for, and besides that, they have no right to be doing anything on our land. I'm going to go talk to them."

"Are you sure? If they're secretly digging around out here maybe we should approach them at a safer time." Jason was trying to just give a suggestion, but his tone made it clear that he was pleading with his chief. This was not the time to walk into a group of unknown men who were brazen enough to be working on someone else's property without permission.

The chief was too upset to be reasoned with, however. His anger over the audacity of these people forced him to start walking over to the pit. Jason tried to stop him but Ron refused, so Jason leapt back down under cover and watched helplessly as Ron approached the group. He almost got close enough to touch them before they even realized Ron was there.

"Hey, who are you?" growled the scruffy man.

"I should be asking you that question!" Ron sneered back at him. "This is our land. What do you think you are doing digging around on our inheritance? You have no right to be here!"

"I don't know what you are talking about. Our company said it's just fine. We're simply following orders."

"I need to speak with your superiors. This is Reserve land and none of you should be here. Give me their names and leave immediately!" Ron's face was now twisted with anger. He was normally a calm, peaceful man but this invasion made him feel more anger than he ever had before. He was so intent on yelling at this man that he didn't even notice one of the others circle around behind him. Before he could get any kind of an answer out of 'Scruffy', he felt a sudden sharp pain on the back of his head, then lost all sense of feeling. He didn't even feel his body thump the ground as he fell over unconscious.

Jason had seen the man circle around behind Ron and jumped out from his hiding spot. He ran quickly and quietly, desperately wanting to reach them before any damage could be done. But he wasn't even half way there when he saw Ron hit the ground. Without thinking, he cried out, and then realized his mistake as the men turned to chase after him. Jason tore off back into the forest with six brutes close behind him. In the darkness he had a hard time seeing the trail. There was a sudden drop in the ground and he lost his balance as the momentum caused his body to start flying ahead faster than his feet. He stumbled, then tripped over a rock and dived into the ground, trying to protect his head with his arms. His elbow shattered when it hit a large rock, taking the brunt of the impact. He let out a piercing cry of agony.

In a moment the six men were on top of him. One of them shined a flashlight in his face while two others scrambled to get him to his feet. Jason screeched again as they pulled on his battered arm, and then went limp. The pain was too much and he passed out.

"Drag him back to the other one," said the man with the flashlight.

Two men grabbed Jason's feet and literally dragged him across the rocky ground back to the pit. By the time they got there Jason's back and head were scraped and bloodied. They dropped his legs beside Ron and the scruffy man looked him over.

"What do we do with them Dylan?" asked the one with the flashlight.

"Two of you tie them up and take them with the rest of the stuff to storage tonight. The rest of you fan out and search the area. Make sure no one else was with them. Got it?"

"Got it."

The men scurried away to do what they were told and Dylan pulled out a satellite phone. A woman answered on the other end with no effort to hide the irritation in her voice.

"Who is it?" she demanded. "It's late!"

"It's Dylan. I know it's late but there's something you should know."

"What is it?"

"Two guys showed up here tonight. I don't know how they even knew we were here but one of them started ranting about how we're on their land before we knocked him out. The other one made a run for it but we got him too."

"How could this happen Dylan? Did someone follow you?" she blasted.

"No way! I don't know how they found us. Maybe they saw the activity. I tried to tell you we should stick to running at night."

"Oh, so now you're giving the orders! That's funny, I thought I hired you! Look. The orders were given from the top. We have demands to meet and this is how we're going to meet them. If you don't like that, I would be happy to pass it along to the boss. At the same time I think I might also mention how you were responsible for that mess on Cedar Narrows Road. What do you think?"

Dylan clenched his teeth. This woman was a thorn in his side but he had no choice but to obey her.

"I told the guys to throw the men in storage tonight. What do you want me to do with them after that?"

"I'll get back to you," she replied with a satisfied tone. She hung up and shook her head. Dylan was a good henchman but she was quickly tiring of his attitude. Walking over to the cabinet she pulled out some brandy and poured herself a generous glass. She sat and slowly sipped on the brandy, mulling over their new predicament. Perhaps she should inform the boss. She quickly dismissed that thought. He hated to deal with all the details. That was why he hired her. She would make sure all the bumps in the road were removed and cleaned up. Instead, she came up with a solution.

The woman grabbed the phone and dialled.

"Hello?"

"Hi Jack. How's it going?"

"What do you want?" came the sharp reply.

"We need to meet, now. You know where."

CHAPTER 13

Jack locked the door behind him then walked hurriedly over to his car. He started it up and tore off down the street. A block down the street, Justin, Nicole and Gabriel watched him depart and prepared to follow. Justin waited until Jack turned the corner before he pulled out. He maintained a comfortable distance so as not to spook Jack, but Jack was too annoyed to notice if anyone was following him.

Jack was driving along the river which forms the border between the U.S. and Canada. He was driving upstream, toward the point where Rainy Lake flows into Rainy River. Nicole told Justin to stop when Jack turned off to go into Pither's Point Park.

"What's wrong?" Justin asked.

"If we follow him in there right away he'll know something's up. Let's keep going ahead and we can get in another way."

Justin complied, driving across the bridge that went over the railroad tracks, then he turned right at the next street. He kept going toward the water at the end of the street. They noticed a restaurant and hotel sitting at the water's edge, and to the right there was a sign posted advertising the park.

"Let's park in the hotel's lot and walk in," Nicole suggested. "Gabriel, you should probably stay here out of sight. We'll be back soon."

Gabriel nodded his head and hunkered down in the back seat. Nicole and Justin quietly got out and started across into the park. They followed the road past the campsites, headed back toward the other entrance Jack had gone into.

"What's in here?" Justin whispered.

"Just a few campsites, some swings and bathrooms, a tower overlooking the town and the old fort."

"Fort?" he inquired.

"That's right. How do you think it got the name Fort Frances? Years ago the Voyageurs built a fort here and it still stands. I bet Jack is meeting someone inside it. No one would bother them in there at night."

Before long, they reached a large clearing in which Justin could see the fort. It was dimly lit by the street lights on the road circling the campsites.

The fort was obviously quite old. Behind a fortification of stakes, there was a courtyard surrounded by living quarters once used to support the trading post. There were towers on the corners and walkways between them to allow men to shoot at enemies from behind the stakes. In front of the fort stood Jack's car alongside another one. Both cars appeared to be empty.

Nicole and Justin stealthily sneaked up to the large main door and carefully opened it enough to squeeze through, closing it behind them.

Voices could be heard coming from one of the buildings inside. Nicole recognized Jack's voice right away but she did not recognize the woman's. She motioned for Justin to follow her as she slowly crept around the backside of the buildings. There was a small alley of sorts behind the area where Jack was talking. Nicole assumed they had entered through the courtyard and did not want to bump into them. They managed to get behind the room Jack was in and could clearly hear them talking through the window, which was nothing more than a hole now. Inside, a lantern lit up the room while Jack and the mystery woman spoke. The woman's face wasn't visible through the window.

The woman was giving instructions to Jack. "We need to move more product tomorrow night. I want you to go the storage facility with Dylan and the others at midnight."

"Ok, fine. Back to business as usual," he responded.

"Not quite. There's been a complication."

"What? Another one?" Jack whined.

"Yes, and I need you to help Dylan clean it up," the woman barked.

"What now?"

"Two Indians showed up at the Reserve location tonight and started something. Dylan knocked them out and said he'll tie them up in storage tonight. I need you two to disappear them."

"Are you insane? You expect me to be able to keep covering up these bodies? It was bad enough that John had to die but the bodies just keep piling up!"

"And whose fault is that?" she retorted.

Jack's eyes almost popped out of his head and his nostrils flared with anger. He snarled at the woman and said, "The only reason John is dead is because your guy, Dylan, lost control. We were just checking on things out at the island when John came up onshore to take a leak. It was Dylan who flipped out when he saw John and chased after him and drowned him. By the time I caught up John was dead. I told him John hadn't seen anything and all he would have had to do was spin a tail about fishing and wait for the guy to leave. Instead he drowns him!"

"I'm aware of the story Jack! I was referring to your sloppy cover-up!" she shouted back.

"Hey, it was a good plan. There were no marks on the body. All we had to do was dump the boat and body and make it look like an accidental drowning. You know what? It worked. I talked to Nicole and she was closing the case. Then you go ahead and start resuming activity the next night! I told you we should lay low for a while so that no one would be suspicious of anything, but you start moving stuff again in the middle of the day. It's your fault that we had to stage a prison break and take care of Gabriel, Nicole and Frank. Now I have to work a miracle to cover up two dead cops, and two dead Indians! How am I supposed to avoid detection when we keep killing people?"

"That's enough! You know I have demands to meet. I didn't have time to wait around. Now we can't afford to have people snooping around the Reserve site so we have to get rid of the Indians. Make sure it's clean. Now, are we clear of the cop bodies?"

"Yes," Jack spouted back. The woman simply raised her eyebrows waiting for an explanation. "We cleaned up the mess at Johnson's house so no one will ask any questions about that. Gabriel and Nicole will be discovered in the next few days as having been the unfortunate victims of an accidental explosion. The findings will indicate that the propane tank at the cabin the mill uses up at Rabbit Lake leaked and sadly blew up the cabin along with the two people inside. Why they were there together will remain a mystery. As for Frank, he is in the bottom of a swamp nobody ever goes to and he will forever be a missing person. I'll see to it the detachment wastes time searching for him to distract them from the island."

"Excellent. Just make sure the next two are cleaned up properly and we should be fine. And be sure that everyone stays away from the Johnson house from now on. I don't want any more interference from anyone and we can't afford to have our guys spotted there snooping around. We've been running this operation smoothly for a while and I want it to go back to that. Am I making myself clear?"

"Yes, fine."

"Good. Then I'll talk to you in a couple of days. I want good news. Now let's go."

The woman walked out into the courtyard followed by Jack and the lantern. Nicole and Justin waited quietly for them to leave. They heard both cars start up and take off. Once the sounds faded into the distance the two carefully made their way back to the large gate and slipped outside the fort. They didn't say a word on their walk back. Both of them kept an eye out for any movements as they worked their way back to Gabriel. Once they were inside they simply looked at each other and breathed deeply. Nicole felt like she had been holding her breath the whole time.

"What happened?" Gabriel inquired.

"What didn't happen?" Justin said with a sigh.

"What do you mean?" Gabriel stated, confused.

Nicole informed him, "You were right when you said it seemed suspicious that John drowned. We overheard Jack speaking with a woman who is obviously calling the shots here. She has Jack and some guy named Dylan cleaning up her messes, and who knows how many others moving some kind of product for her. Hey, Justin, what do you think the product is?"

Before Justin could respond, Gabriel jumped in and asked, "How do you know John was murdered?"

"Jack explained to the woman that he and the other guy were out on that island we went to together. John pulled up with the boat to go to the bathroom and that other guy freaked out and drowned him.

Jack tried to cover it up by making it look like a boating accident. I'm sorry Gabriel," Nicole said sympathetically.

Gabriel just sat back in his seat and went silent. He couldn't help but imagine what it must have been like for John. He could feel the hands on him, holding him under the water. It made him start to cry a little at the thought of John thrashing around fighting for air. Before he got too carried away, Gabriel stopped himself. He knew that imagining John's death wasn't going to help right now. He had to concentrate on helping catch the killers. Just at that moment Justin spoke up.

"I think they're moving drugs," he said.

"Really?" Gabriel responded.

"It makes sense," added Nicole. "What else could they be shipping around that they would need to hide and that would make them enough money they can buy off police and hire mercenaries to kill anyone who gets in their way? I can't think of anything else around here that would do that. Also, with being right on the American border, there are an awful lot of drugs being smuggled across the border here. There are only two things that don't add up to me."

"Like what?" Justin inquired.

"Well, for starters, why would they haul the drugs out to an island to hide it? I know it's a good hiding place but it seems like a lot of unnecessary work. Why would they drive it to the landing, transfer it into a boat, drive to the island to hide, then have to repeat the process to remove it? They could just stick it in a cabin somewhere and save the whole water issue."

"Good question," Justin pondered.

"I think I know why," Gabriel said slowly.

The two officers turned to look at him inquisitively. He offered his idea.

"Robson Lake actually flows into the north end of Rainy Lake through a narrow opening. Not many people know where. Suppose they were smuggling the drugs in by boat. There are all kinds of boats on Rainy Lake and the police can't check them all. So if they loaded up on the American side of the lake they could zip across the imaginary border undetected, boat up to the entrance to Robson Lake, and quietly deposit the drugs on the island until they were ready to move them. It's a perfect setup because my house is the only place there and the lake is big enough that I wouldn't normally notice them doing anything. Everywhere else there are all kinds of cabins and boaters to worry about. Only a few people use the landing so if they moved the drugs at night no one would ever know."

"Makes sense to me," Justin said.

"Me too," Nicole agreed.

"The only thing is that we were on that island and found nothing," Gabriel said with a puzzled expression.

"They must have it well hidden. We would probably have to catch them in the act to find it," Nicole stated. "We'll just have to do that tomorrow night."

"Tomorrow night?" Gabriel asked.

"Yes, they're going to be there to move the drugs at midnight. We probably can't stop them, but we can find out where it's being stored and where they are shipping it. I just have one more question," Nicole responded.

"What's that?" inquired Justin.

"What does the First Nations Reserve have to do with all of this?"

"Is that where the drugs are going?" Gabriel asked.

"I don't know. He mentioned two men from the Reserve snooping around something and they are going to make them disappear. They must have seen some part of the operation they shouldn't have. It sounded like they are on that island with the drugs," Justin explained.

"We should head back to Gabriel's and rest. Then we can come up with a plan tomorrow," Nicole suggested.

"I thought it wasn't safe to go back there?" Gabriel said, confused.

"The woman told Jack that no one was to go there. She's afraid of someone spotting them. They cleaned up the house to make it look like nothing happened so that there would be no one suspecting foul play over our death at the cabin. They don't want anything being tied to them. So, we now know that your house is a safe place to hide from the bad guys," Nicole explained.

Justin drove out of the parking lot and headed back out toward Gabriel's house.

"Well, at least I'll be able to sleep in my bed again," Gabriel said.

CHAPTER 14

The next day, after a much needed rest, the three put together a plan for observing the island. Gabriel filled up the fuel tanks on his boat and checked that everything was in working order. Nicole and Justin checked their weapons and ensured they had light surveillance equipment and flashlights ready. Included in the equipment were night vision binoculars and wireless headsets for communication.

After loading the boat they headed across the lake toward the island. It was a gamble heading there in the open like this but they were confident that no one would be around until midnight. As they approached the island, Gabriel veered away from the dock where they had seen the three men previously and maneuvered around to the other side of the island where they would be out of view. They pulled up the boat to shore and tied it off to a tree. After unloading their gear, they headed back to the opposite side of the island to find a good vantage point from which they could observe things while staying hidden. Nicole and Gabriel sat to the South and Justin went to the North, just to ensure they didn't miss anything.

Hours later, close to midnight, Justin was stifling a yawn when he heard the sound of a boat echoing across the water. "Someone's coming," he whispered into his headset. Gabriel and Nicole sat up when they heard his report. Before long, they could hear the boat as well. They waited impatiently while the boat slowly approached, with bright lights shining on the water. As it came closer they realized a second boat was following behind. Nicole looked through the night vision binoculars and gasped a little.

"What's wrong?" whispered Gabriel.

"It looks like the first boat is towing a small barge or something. They must have a huge shipment of drugs in there. I can't believe it."

They watched while the boats eased over to the dock and tied off. Huge lights from the boats lit up the whole dock and part of the shoreline. Four men stepped off the tow-boat. Two more men came from the other boat, one of them with a rifle slung over his shoulder. They watched as the others went to work. Two men went to the barge, which was piled high with some kind of bins, and started moving some bins onto the dock. Meanwhile, two others headed toward land with headlamps on. Once they touched the ground they turned and followed the shoreline going north.

"Justin, two guys are headed your way. I'm losing sight of them," Nicole quietly stated.

"I see them. I'll keep an eye on them while you guys watch the dock," he responded.

Justin remained still in the darkness while he watched the two men walk toward him. He couldn't quite tell what they were doing but it almost seemed like they were pushing brush away while walking slowly along the water's edge. He wanted to move closer but hesitated since they kept moving in his direction. With about fifty yards remaining between Justin and the men they stopped, and turned inland. After a short distance they moved a high pile of debris and started walking back toward the dock while pushing something.

"Guys, they're headed back in your direction and are pushing something along the ground. I can't tell what they're up to," Justin stated.

Gabriel and Nicole watched as the men re-appeared pushing something up to the dock. They then went to pick up the bins placed on the dock. The bins were so heavy that they required one man on each end and it seemed like the men struggled a little with the load. Slowly, they carried the bins back to the shore and piled them up there.

"It looks like they're putting those bins on some kind of dolly," Gabriel observed.

After loading up a few bins the two men began pushing them following the path they were on before. One of the men supervising followed behind them as they turned inland and disappeared.

"Hey Justin. Can you see where they are going?" asked Nicole.

"Not really. They walked a little ways and have kind of disappeared. I'll try to get closer."

Justin began to quietly move closer to where he lost sight of the men. He could hear the voices of the men working on the dock and the thud of bins being banged around. A twig snapped under his foot and he froze. His heart began pounding as he waited to hear someone start shouting or firing bullets his way. While he tried to catch his breath, he looked toward the dock. The men were still working as though they heard nothing. And there seemed to be no sign of the others who had traveled onto the island. He let out a sigh of relief as it appeared the sound went unnoticed.

Cautiously, Justin made his way as close as he dared to the spot the men disappeared. The whole area was lit up so he stayed back in the darkness to watch. He could see on the ground two rails, almost like train tracks following the shore from the dock to the North, then curving inland. But from his vantage point he couldn't see where they lead. He looked back at the dock to see if anyone was watching and, sure enough, one of the men was standing there carefully observing the whole area. He seemed to be standing guard and would likely spot Justin if he stepped into the light at all.

"Nicole, I can see two rails on the ground that they must be using to wheel a cart along. I think they managed to camouflage it all. I still can't see where they're taking everything but there's a guard keeping an eye out so we'll have to hang back to avoid being spotted."

"Ok. Should we stay to keep watching or take off?" she asked.

"I would sure like to get a look at what they're moving. Why don't we sit tight and get a closer look when they leave?" Justin replied.

"Will do," was the response.

They quietly stayed where they were for a few hours while the men finished unloading the bins and hauling them onto the island. They watched while the men returned the camouflage to hide their tracks and boarded the boats to leave. The lights turned away from shore and were trained on the water ahead of them as they moved away from the dock and headed back the way they came.

Once the boats seemed far enough away, Justin turned on his flashlight and moved down to where the tracks turned inland from the shore. He lifted the items used to camouflage the tracks and waited for Nicole and Gabriel to get to him. Once they were together, they began revealing the track while slowly moving deeper onto the island. Each of them felt a little deflated as they headed along a ridge and came to the spot where the tracks ended at the ridge wall. They just seemed to stop at a dead end. Puzzled, they started looking around to see if they missed something.

Gabriel looked more closely at the ridge wall and brushed aside some vines to reveal a sort of door carefully camouflaged to remain hidden. He felt around it and found with some force he could slide the wooden frame sideways, revealing an entryway into a cave. Just inside, a sort of trolley was revealed.

"They must have been wheeling the items into this cave to store," commented Gabriel.

The three stepped inside the cave while shining their lights about the area. Though the opening was only slightly larger than an entryway on a typical home, they could tell the cave was sizeable. Although, it was hard to really see everything in the darkness, even with their flashlights. Nicole spotted a bin, stepped over to it and started to pry the lid off. Justin helped her. Meanwhile, Gabriel shone a light back toward the entrance and something flashed, reflecting his light. He walked over to it while the other two kept working at the bins. There was a switch attached to the cave wall. Gabriel hesitated a moment, unsure of what would happen if he touched it. Curiosity overcame him and he reached out to flip it.

'Click,' was all he heard, and then nothing. His shoulders dropped partly from relief and partly from disappointment. He began to wonder why there would be a switch installed there that does nothing, when he noticed a gentle rumbling sound coming from deep inside the cavern. At first he was happy that the switch had done something, but a sick feeling began to tighten his stomach as he realized that he had no idea what he had just awakened.

"Shh," he said to Nicole and Justin. "Do you hear that?"

They stopped banging on the bins for a moment to listen. Their eyes widened when both of them could hear the same rumbling sound as Gabriel. Their imaginations began to run wild as they tried to determine the source of the sound. But in a few brief seconds, lights in the ceiling of the cave began to flicker on. The switch had engaged a small, quiet generator that was feeding power to the lights. More and more lights came on and they all gasped as an enormous room, with a thirty foot high ceiling, was revealed.

They had discovered one of the largest caves of the region, here on this isolated island, and it was being filled up with sealed bins.

"Oh my…" said Nicole, her mouth gaping open. "There has to be thousands of bins stacked in here! How is this possible?"

"I have no idea," commented Gabriel. He was equally in shock.

Nicole began to attack the bin she had been prying open and, aided by the clear lights, she tore off the lid.

"Is that what I think it is?" Justin inquired as he reached into the bin.

"It can't be!" replied Nicole. "All these bins are full of…"

"Gold!" said a voice from behind the three of them. "They're full of gold!"

CHAPTER 15

Nicole, Justin and Gabriel spun around at the sound of an unexpected voice. Standing at the cave entrance, guns drawn, was Jack Rudiger flanked by Dylan. Both of them wore a menacing scowl.

"I have to give you credit Nicole. You are the luckiest person I know! Twice now you've evaded us, even making us think you were dead," Jack sneered with a slight grin.

"What can I say, I'm a high achiever!" she sarcastically quipped.

Jack chuckled and replied, "Well, I'm sorry to say your lucky streak ends tonight. You know, we had considered bringing you into our little enterprise here. You're a talented officer, but just too clean... too perfect. I knew you would never consider it. And I guess I was right. It's unfortunate to waste such talent...such beauty."

Jack took a moment to ogle Nicole with a filthy look in his eyes.

"Don't talk to her that way!" blurted Gabriel as he took a step forward.

"Awww! I'm sorry. I didn't realize you two were an item," Jack condescendingly responded as he pointed his weapon at Gabriel. "Come on then, big man. You think you can stop me?"

Gabriel stopped moving and clenched his fists. He was a calm man normally but right now, he wanted to give Jack the thrashing of a lifetime. Nicole gently touched Gabriel's arm. He looked at her as she shook her head slightly. Gabriel stepped back while Jack roared with laughter. He was enjoying tormenting them, like a cat that tortures a mouse before killing it.

Jack's tone became abrupt. "As much as I would like to keep this little reunion going, I have deadlines to meet. Dylan…why don't you take care of these two gentlemen in here and dump their bodies in the back end of the cave with the others. Nicole and I are going to take a stroll to the boat. Join us there when you're done and we'll take care of her after. I have something special in mind for her."

"With pleasure," Dylan creepily responded with a crooked smile.

Nicole looked at Gabriel with tears in her eyes. Both of them felt torn apart inside. This was not the end either one had envisioned. How could this happen? What could they do to stop it? Jack grabbed Nicole by the arm and tugged at her to walk. Gabriel held his breath as he looked at her, then back at Dylan, who was jabbing him with a pistol. He desperately wanted to find a way to save Nicole, but how?

Jack's laughter echoed through the cave as he and Nicole disappeared out the entryway. Gabriel and Justin looked at each other as they moved deeper into the cave between the stacked bins, with Dylan close behind. Suddenly, all three paused when they heard the generator sputter. The lights flickered and went out, darkness enveloping them once again. Justin didn't waste a moment, leaping on Dylan and grappling for the gun. Gabriel heard them fighting and darted through the stacks of bins to get away from them. Blindly, he fumbled through the darkness and finally ducked behind a tower of bins. He flinched as a gunshot blasted. Someone squealed in pain, but the scuffling continued. Two more shots were fired quickly. Everything went silent.

"Gabriel…where are you?" Justin called out.

Gabriel remained quiet, not knowing what to do. He listened as the sound of something being dragged began to be heard. There was someone breathing heavily, smacking into bins and dragging something along the cave floor. Then the beam of a flashlight began flashing around the cave. Again Justin called out to Gabriel. Gabriel carefully and silently began moving in the direction of the light. When he got close, he held his breath and slowly peeked around a stack of bins. He saw Justin holding the flashlight and a gun, standing next to Dylan's body. Actually, Justin was leaning against a pile of bins as he was clearly hurt.

"I'm here," Gabriel responded in a hushed tone. "I'm ok. What happened?"

Justin looked up at him and replied, "He shot me in the leg but I managed to overtake him. I think he's dead."

Gabriel stepped over to Dylan while Justin kept the gun trained on his body. Gabriel could see a pool of blood forming underneath Dylan. He flipped Dylan onto his back and his lifeless eyes made it clear he was gone. Both men sighed with relief. Justin slid down to the ground to rest, wincing from the pain in his leg. Gabriel rushed over to help.

"Stop. I'll be ok for a bit. But I can't run right now. You have to go help Nicole," Justin urged.

"What do I do? I'm not trained for this!" stated Gabriel.

"Here…take the gun. You'll need it. The safety is off. Have you ever used a gun before?"

"I've used rifles and shotguns for hunting but never a handgun."

"The principles are the same. Just line him up in the sights and squeeze the trigger. Aim for his chest, it's a bigger target. Hold onto it with both hands if you can when you shoot. Now go!" Justin commanded.

Gabriel took the gun in his hands. It was heavier than he thought it would be. He picked up one of the other flashlights and paused for a moment. This was so surreal. His head was spinning at the thought of shooting a human being. Hunting animals was one thing, but killing a person was something he never thought he could be capable of.

"Go!" Justin shouted.

That shout brought him to his senses and he began to sprint for the entrance. Gabriel burst out of the cave and headed for the dock. Jack had pushed Nicole into the stern of the boat, and was starting to untie it from the dock, when he noticed the bouncing beam of the flashlight heading toward them.

"Looks like Dylan took care of your friends," snarled Jack as he stepped onto the boat and glared at Nicole. "Don't worry. It won't be too much longer for you."

Jack stepped over to the controls and checked the gauges. When he heard the footfalls coming down the dock, nearing the boat, he fired up the motor. He could feel the man step onto the boat and prepared to drive away. Nicole had been watching Jack's movements looking for her chance to jump him, but decided not to try it with Dylan approaching them. When 'Dylan' stepped aboard she was surprised to see him thrusting a gun toward her, with the handle facing her. She almost gasped when she looked up, confused. It was Gabriel! Despite her momentary hesitation, she grabbed the gun and pointed it at Jack.

"I told you, that's no way to treat a lady!" barked Gabriel as he tightened his right hand into a fist.

Jack's head snapped up, and he only began to turn around when Gabriel's fist landed on his jaw. Jack fell against the side of the boat and it started to rock erratically. Gabriel lost his balance and tried to steady himself. Jack quickly came up with his gun ready, but Nicole was faster and fired first. Jack fell hard onto the floor of the boat, his gun splashing into the water. Nicole and Gabriel stepped over to the dock while Nicole watched Jack's movements. Jack sat up slightly, breathing with difficulty and leaning against a seat. He winced, then smiled at the two of them.

"You truly are the luckiest person I know," he said weakly to Nicole. "You probably think you've won. But you're far from it."

"What do you mean? Who else is involved? Where did that gold come from and why are you hiding it?" Nicole demanded to know.

Jack smirked and sputtered, "You…have…no…idea…who…you're up against. They…will…destroy…you."

His body went limp and he slid sideways, collapsing onto the bottom of the boat. Nicole carefully stepped back over and checked if he was still alive. She looked up at Gabriel and shook her head. As tears flowed down her face, she leaped back onto the dock into Gabriel's embrace. For a moment, the world stood still as the two kissed. Both were in turmoil inside. The emotional toll of being on the run, nearly dying, and fighting their attraction for one another all combined into one passionate kiss. It took so much energy, both of them had to pause to catch their breath.

"I thought you were gone for sure when I heard the gunshots," Nicole whispered. "How did you…?"

"It was Justin. He overpowered the other guy…" Gabriel began to explain. He stopped and exclaimed, "We have to go back to help him! He's hurt."

Gabriel took Nicole by the hand and they ran back toward shore. They followed the trail to the cave and ran inside to find Justin waiting where Gabriel had left him.

"Justin! I'm so glad you're ok!" Nicole beamed.

"I'm alive, but don't know about ok," he tried to joke with a slight smile. "I don't think I can walk. My leg took a bullet."

"Let me see," Nicole responded as she tried to check out the wound.

"Shhh," Gabriel hushed.

All three went silent as they listened. Nicole and Justin weren't sure what Gabriel heard and wondered why he told them to be quiet. But Gabriel could hear it again and quietly took a few steps deeper into the cave. It sounded like whispers coming from deep within. Nicole got up and followed behind Gabriel while Justin watched them tiptoe away. As they got closer to the sound Nicole began to hear what Gabriel picked up on. She was amazed he heard it at all before. They carefully pointed the flashlight around corners of the stacked bins looking for the source of the sound. As they neared the back of the cave they could make out words.

"Please…help…me…" someone whispered over and over.

The two couldn't help but feel like this was some kind of trap as they got closer. The hairs on their necks were standing on end. Their breathing became rapid as adrenaline began pumping even harder through them. They could tell they were almost on top of the person making the sound when Gabriel stopped moving. Silently he signalled Nicole to ask if they should keep going. She thought a moment, then nodded slowly. They moved forward and poked their heads around the next corner. There a man lay still, eyes closed, with his lips moving ever so slightly as he whispered for help.

As Gabriel and Nicole approached it was evident this man was no threat. He was a bloody mess. Next to him was the generator that had been powering the lights. Farther beyond lay another man.

"It's ok. We're here to help," Nicole assured him. "Who are you? What happened to you?"

The man swallowed hard, and took a deep breath. "My name is Jason," he whispered. "That's my chief. They killed him," he sputtered as tears rolled down his cheeks. Slowly he continued, "They caught us. I tried to get away…but woke up here. I could hardly move. I waited…hoping for help. When I heard them with you, I dragged myself to the generator and turned it off."

Jason started to cough violently. It was clear he was injured beyond recovery. Gabriel and Nicole tried to look him over to see if they could give him any aid.

"I think we'll have to carry him out," suggested Nicole.

Before Gabriel could lift him up, Jason rasped, "Wait…Reserve…Longhorn…" His eyes rolled back in his head, then his head flopped to the side.

"Jason! Can you hear me?" Gabriel pleaded. But there was no response. He and Nicole tried reviving him but to no avail. After a few minutes

Nicole stopped Gabriel from doing chest compressions. She got up and went to check the other body. Then she returned to Gabriel.

"He was right. The other man is dead. We should go," Nicole stated.

"We can't just leave them here like this," Gabriel responded despondently.

"We'll have to for now. We can come back for them later," Nicole said as she touched his shoulder.

Gabriel nodded, stood up, and they both trekked back toward Justin. When they found him again he asked what happened.

"Two more casualties," Nicole told him. "Come on. Let's get you up so we can get out of here."

Gabriel and Nicole helped Justin to his feet and he grunted from the pain. Gabriel supported his weak side as they hobbled all the way back to the end of the dock and into Jack's boat. After setting Justin down on a seat, Gabriel looked down at Jack's body. He started to lift the body and roll it toward the edge of the boat.

"What are you doing?" inquired Nicole.

"I think it's only fair that he get the same treatment he gave John Edberg," Gabriel said, upset.

Nicole nodded agreement. Before Gabriel continued, she went through Jack's pockets and removed his wallet, some keys, and a phone. Then she gestured for Gabriel to continue. He rolled the body over the edge and it splashed into the water. Slowly, it drifted away and sank. Gabriel stepped over to the controls and started the boat. He turned on the lights and drove toward his home. They would have to pick up the boat he stowed on the other side of the island later.

CHAPTER 16

Gabriel hopped out to tie off the boat to his dock. He helped Justin to hobble off the boat and then up to the house. Nicole ran ahead to open the door. They got inside and flopped Justin onto the couch. Gabriel ran to get the first aid kit he kept stocked while Nicole tried to cut away Justin's pant leg. She got the pants off to reveal his bloody wound. It was still bleeding out as she inspected the damage.

She reported, "Justin, I think you're fortunate. It appears the bullet went straight through without hitting a bone or artery. I think if we clean it out and stitch it up you'll be ok."

Gabriel came running back with the first aid kit, some hydrogen peroxide, and a bottle of whiskey. Justin reached over like a flash and took the whiskey, taking a long draw on it.

"Do you have some kind of a needle and thread we could stitch him up with?" Nicole asked Gabriel.

He thought for a moment and replied, "I have some fishing line that might work. I'll have to search for a needle."

"Ok. That'll have to do. I'll boil some water and grab some towels."

Gabriel raced to the garage looking for some thin line. He found a roll, grabbed a box of nitrile gloves he used for oil changes, and ran back to the house trying to remember where he would've put a needle that would work. Hunting through drawers he found a small pack of needles and confirmed one could be threaded with the fishing line. He ran to the kitchen to join Nicole at the stove.

"Perfect," she said. "Now just soak the line in the hot water for a bit to try to clean it. And you should hold the needle in the flame for a while to clean it too. I'll take some towels and start cleaning the wound with peroxide."

Gabriel nodded and got to work. Nicole moved back to Justin and gently lifted his leg a little, placing a towel underneath it. She picked up the peroxide and looked at Justin.

"I'm sorry. This whole thing is probably going to hurt a lot."

"Just do it," Justin urged as he took another pull on the bottle.

Nicole started cleaning the wound as Justin winced and whined from the pain. The whiskey was helping, but wasn't taking away all the pain. By the time she disinfected both sides of the wound, Gabriel came over with the sanitized stitching materials. Nicole stood up and looked at him.

"I don't think I can do the stitching," she whispered.

Gabriel just nodded and sat beside Justin's leg. He put some clean gloves on, picked up the needle, and threaded it. He had already tied a knot in one end of the line to prevent pulling it all the way through the skin. Carefully, he readied himself to start at one end of the wound. He paused to look at Justin. Justin clenched his teeth, then nodded at him. Gabriel steadied his hand, and jabbed the needle through the first piece of the wound. Justin grimaced and screamed through his clenched teeth. He took another drink and barely swallowed before Gabriel poked him again. He tried to quickly stitch up the gap, then tied the same knot he used all the time for tying lures to the line. Nicole cut the excess off and Justin relaxed.

"Ok. Now the other side," she said. "We'll have to turn you a little."

Justin sighed heavily. He thought it was all over. He caught his breath and braced himself to move. They helped him get into the right position and started stitching again. Justin kept drinking, and whining, but Gabriel finished up fairly quickly. He started wiping everything off with the hot towels, poured some more peroxide on the wounds to prevent infection, and applied some large bandages.

"Ok Justin. I've got good news and bad news," Gabriel told him.

"What's the good news?" he asked.

"I think we're all done. We cleaned and stitched the wound the best we could so there hopefully shouldn't be any infection or serious bleeding."

"What's the bad news?" Justin inquired with hesitation in his voice.

"This is the first time I've ever stitched up someone so you're probably going to have some nasty scars left behind."

"That's ok. They always say chicks dig scars right?" Justin responded with a slight grin.

Gabriel and Nicole laughed, glad to see he still had a sense of humour. The whiskey was helping with that. They decided it was best not to move him so they made him comfortable and put a blanket over him. Justin conked out quickly and started to snore. They cleaned everything up and Gabriel grabbed a couple glasses. He picked up the bottle of whiskey and the two of them shared a drink at the table. As Gabriel swallowed he thought to himself that this whiskey had never tasted so good. Nicole broke the silence first.

"Where do you think all that gold came from?" she asked.

"I have no idea," Gabriel admitted. "I know there's gold in this region but that was an unbelievable amount stored in the cave. Why on earth would they store it there? It's not like it's illegal like the drugs we thought they were transporting. Why wouldn't they just refine it and haul it away like every other mine?"

"That's a good question. There must be something underhanded about it. Maybe they stole it from another mine?"

"Maybe…but I don't know of any mines on Rainy Lake they would take it from. And in such large quantities."

"Hmmm. Yeah, how would you manage to steal that much unnoticed from an active mine? This makes even less sense than smuggling drugs."

"What did that guy by the generator say again?" Gabriel asked Nicole.

"Let me think…He said the other man was his chief. They did look to be First Nations. Then he said they got caught and woke up in the cave."

"Right. So do you think he meant they got caught somewhere else and were taken to the cave?"

"Yes I think so. That's what I overheard from Jack and the woman in the fort. But where? And what did they see? Maybe the clue is in his last words. Remember when we tried to pick him up? He stopped us. He must have felt he needed to tell us something important. But I don't understand what he meant by 'reserve longhorn.'"

Gabriel's eyes widened and he jumped up from the table. He ran to the library and Nicole watched, bewildered by his reaction. He came running back with a map, which he spread across the table. Gabriel scanned his eyes across the map and chuckled as he shook his head.

"What is it?" Nicole asked impatiently.

"We are right here," Gabriel responded, pointing to the spot on the map. "Over here is the island where all the gold is stored. Those boats were traveling in the direction of the entrance to Rainy Lake over here. Now if you follow the shore of the lake, here is a First Nations Reserve. See the name of this point here?"

"Longhorn Point!" she answered excitedly. "He was trying to tell us where the gold came from. On the Reserve at Longhorn Point. They must have stumbled upon the mine."

"And if the gold is coming from Reserve land, they are illegally mining for it. Then they are moving it to store somewhere no one would find it until they're ready to transport it to be refined and sold. Since there's no roads going to that spot, and they couldn't build a road without someone noticing, they decided to transport across the lake. They could move on the ice in the winter, and use a barge in the summer. The island is close enough they don't have to travel a long distance with it, and isolated enough to avoid any suspicion."

"If all that gold in the cave came from there then it's certainly enough to motivate them to setup such a large operation," Nicole continued. "What Jack said makes sense. Something of this magnitude can't just be a couple local prospectors. There must be a corrupt organization behind all of this."

They looked at each other and smiled. They had solved the puzzle, at least part of it. They sank in their chairs, processing this.

"What do we do now?" Gabriel inquired.

"It won't be long before someone gets suspicious Jack is missing. When someone goes back to that cave they'll discover the other body. We have to move quickly. We don't know what's at the mine so it's a huge risk to go there on our own. I think we need to identify the woman from the fort. She seems to be in charge. Then we can call in the cavalry."

"Didn't you grab Jack's phone tonight?"

"I did," replied Nicole. "It's locked. He usually opened it up with facial recognition. There was one time…I remember it wouldn't open properly for him once and he had to punch in his code. I think he was so frustrated he didn't notice I could see his screen. What was it…?"

Nicole closed her eyes and tried to visualize the memory. She saw Jack trying to unlock it. He shook the phone. Then it asked for his passcode. 8…5…8…9…1…3. She opened her eyes, picked up the phone and punched in the code. It unlocked.

"Now, how do we figure out who the mystery woman is?" Nicole wondered out loud.

"What if you look at his call history from the night we followed him? Maybe she called shortly before he came out of his house?" Gabriel suggested.

Nicole tried looking and sure enough, there was an incoming call shortly before they had followed Jack that night. She looked at the number and Jack had entered it into his contacts under the name 'Devil'.

"I have a feeling this is the one," she said with a laugh as she showed Gabriel. "After the exchange I overheard inside that fort, I think this well describes the woman, or at least how Jack felt about her."

"Can you look up who owns that?" Gabriel wondered.

"I'd have to go to the office to do that. I don't think that will work. And I don't know who I could ask to do it either."

They both sat silently considering how they could use this phone number to track down the monster running the operation. A light bulb went on in Nicole's mind.

"You know, I think I might know who she is," she said with a smile.

"Really? How? Who?" Gabriel asked excitedly.

Nicole answered, "When I went to talk to John Edberg's wife, Wanda, she told me that she was involved with precious metals and prospectors for work. I later checked that out and it's true. She would be in a good position to be involved with a gem company for selling the gold."

"Wanda? Really? But I thought you said you didn't recognize her at the fort? And wouldn't this also mean she would have been involved in John's murder?"

"I never actually saw the woman's face at the fort. And she could've altered her voice when I spoke to her. The husband's murder wasn't planned. It happened without her involvement. Plus, honestly it didn't sound like they had the best relationship. And you'd be surprised how many times one mate becomes violent with the other. Maybe it didn't actually bother her that much. Or maybe she just had to live with it once it was done."

Gabriel raised his eyebrows and replied, "I can't come up with anything better. I guess I didn't really know Wanda very well anyway. How do we proceed?"

"I think we should leave Justin here to rest. He'll be fine, and we need to move fast. Let's drive to Fort Frances to Wanda's home and confront her. I think that's the only move we have right now."

They checked on Justin one last time, grabbed their things and turned out the lights. Nicole offered to drive, so Gabriel tried to rest on the long trip to

Fort Frances.

CHAPTER 17

Gabriel looked out over Rainy Lake as they drove across the causeway that stretched over the lake, just east of Fort Frances. The sun was starting to peek above the horizon sending streaks of beautiful orange and yellow colors across the sky. He hadn't managed to sleep at all. The excitement from the night before was still keeping him awake. Plus, there were so many questions spinning through his mind.

Nicole entered the town, and turned onto the street where Wanda lived. They pulled up a few doors down the block and turned off the car.

"Looks like she's up," stated Gabriel, pointing at the light that was on inside.

Nicole responded, "That's good. When we go inside, just let me do the talking. Here, take Jack's phone. I have it unlocked and ready to dial 'Devil'. When I give you the signal, dial the number and she'll know she's caught when her phone rings."

"Ok. Let's hope this works."

The two stepped outside in the brisk morning air. It felt nice actually. Gabriel found it like a slap in the face to wake him up a little. Nicole knocked on the door. The house was quiet. She knocked again, more loudly this time. Someone stirred inside. They could hear her walking to the door. The door opened to reveal Wanda Edberg still dressed in a night robe. She paused for a moment, with a confused look on her face.

"Officer…?" Wanda's voice trailed off as she tried to recall the name.

"Nicole Edouard, ma'am."

"Right. It's awfully early. What are you doing here?" Wanda inquired. She was still rubbing her eyes.

"I apologize for the early hour Mrs. Edberg. There's an important matter we need to discuss with you. Can we come in?"

Wanda looked at Gabriel, then back to Nicole. She shrugged her shoulders and waved them in. They stepped into the living room. Wanda sat on a plush chair while Gabriel and Nicole remained standing. Nicole glanced down at the coffee table and saw Wanda's cell phone sitting there. Wanda took a sip from her coffee mug.

"I'm sorry. Would you guys like some coffee?" Wanda offered.

"No, thank you," Nicole replied.

"Wait a minute. You knew John," Wanda said looking at Gabriel. "You're not a police officer."

Gabriel felt an anxious knot develop instantly in his stomach. He tried desperately not to let it show. He didn't know what to say and didn't want to ruin this moment.

"No, he's not an officer," Nicole replied calmly. "This is Gabriel Johnson. He's the one who discovered your husband after he drowned."

"Oh, ok. So, are the two of you here because you have more information about my husband?"

"Actually, we're here because I have reason to believe you have more information about your husband. It seems there's some details you left out of our last discussion!"

"What? No, I told you everything I know," Wanda blurted out with bewilderment.

Gabriel observed her reaction closely and couldn't help but feel Wanda seemed genuinely confused by the accusation. He thought to himself that she must just be a good actress. He nervously glanced at the phone in his hand to make sure it was still unlocked. It was ready to dial. He looked back at Nicole to await her signal.

"Is that so? Let me see if I can refresh your memory. Does the name Jack Rudiger ring a bell?" Nicole squinted as she said it, watching for Wanda's reaction.

"No," she replied slowly, again sounding confused. "Should it?"

Nicole turned her head and simply nodded at Gabriel. He lifted the phone and dialled 'Devil'. He put it to his ear instinctively, and heard it start to ring. Both Gabriel and Nicole looked down at Wanda's phone waiting for it to light up and start ringing. But as the call continued, Wanda's phone remained silent.

"Well good morning Jack," spoke a voice into Gabriel's ear. "It's excessively early for a phone call isn't it? Or did you just have such great news for me that you couldn't wait to call?"

Gabriel's eyes widened and he looked at Nicole. His mouth gaped open but he said nothing. Nicole realized someone had answered and gestured for him to respond. Wanda looked on, utterly disoriented by this development. She had no idea what was happening this morning and didn't know what to say in response to how Nicole and Gabriel were behaving.

"Jack? Can you hear me?" came the voice again.

Gabriel rubbed his free hand on the mic of the phone hoping to disguise his voice and said, "Yes I hear you."

"Your reception is terrible. I can hardly hear you. Why did you call?"

"Not over the phone. I think we should meet," Gabriel replied, desperately hoping it would work. It was all he could think to do.

"Did you say meet? Fine…the usual place. I can be there in thirty minutes."

"Perfect," Gabriel agreed and hung up.

Nicole stared at Gabriel waiting to find out what the person said. Gabriel looked at her, then glanced back at Wanda who looked totally dumbfounded.

"I apologize for the intrusion, Mrs. Edberg. Thank you for your time. We'll be on our way," Nicole rapidly stated while pushing Gabriel to the door.

Wanda didn't respond. She just sat in her chair, dazed.

When Gabriel and Nicole jumped back inside the car, he explained the brief conversation with 'Devil'. They briefly rejoiced at how fortunate they were to have arranged the meeting. Now they needed to think carefully about how to proceed, but there was little time to plan. Nicole started the car and drove to the spot they had parked a couple days prior, near Pither's Point Park. On the way, they hatched a plan on what to do inside the old fort.

CHAPTER 18

'Devil' parked next to the old fort. She stepped out and surveyed the area. All was still. No one was anywhere close. She usually preferred to have these meetings under cover of darkness, but it was barely light out and there were some vital matters to discuss. Jack's car wasn't around yet. She tucked a gun in her belt at the back, under her coat. Now that she was ready, she strolled to the fort and stepped inside. As she began to head across the little courtyard for their meeting room, 'Devil' sensed something was amiss. She paused, then heard the familiar click of a gun hammer behind her.

"Let me see your hands!" Nicole barked in her official tone.

'Devil' raised her hands and remained still.

"Turn around…slowly. Keep your hands up!"

'Devil' turned as ordered. She looked at Nicole defiantly. Nicole couldn't remember if she had ever met the woman. She had the look of a venomous serpent. Her eyes were cold, fearless, and penetrating. She appeared to be calculating when to strike, much like a viper preparing to launch. Gabriel stepped out from his hiding place and approached.

"Check under her coat for a weapon," Nicole told him.

Gabriel stepped toward 'Devil' but stopped when she turned her head toward him.

"Keep your hands off me!" she hissed.

Gabriel froze. Her eyes had murder in them. And the way she spoke, it was as if venom was dripping from her tongue. In that moment, Gabriel could see why Jack called her 'Devil'. What a hideous woman!

"You're not giving the orders here!" Nicole shouted at her. "Turn around again."

The woman stabbed Nicole with her eyes, but complied. Nicole kept her gun trained on the woman and slowly approached from behind. She patted her back and felt the outline of a gun. She reached under the coat and pulled it free, then backed up and handed it to Gabriel.

"Now hold still," Nicole commanded as she prepared her handcuffs.

Nicole pulled one of the woman's hands down behind her and placed a cuff on the wrist. She then reached for the other hand and started to pull it down. When she was just about to place the cuff on the second wrist, the woman rapidly twisted and jerked her elbow up, catching Nicole on the side of her head. Nicole went down and the woman bolted for the fort entrance.

"Stop!" cried Gabriel, trying to point the gun in his hands.

The woman paused at the door to look back at Gabriel. An evil grin formed on her lips when she could see he wouldn't be able to pull the trigger. She ran through the door, heading for her car.

"We have to stop her!" gasped Nicole.

The two of them pursued the woman. Nicole couldn't believe what happened. In her experience on the Force, she had never seen someone move like that to resist arrest. They came running out of the fort in time to hear the car fire up. The woman stomped on the accelerator, flinging gravel and dust behind the car. Nicole ran to where she could get a clean shot. She aimed carefully, hoping to be able to fire before the car got too far away. A front tire of the car exploded when Nicole's bullet struck its target. The car swung wildly, pulling to the embankment by the beach. Before 'Devil' could correct, her car flew over the edge and fell about six feet, slamming into the sand.

Nicole and Gabriel raced over to the beach to see what happened. As they came up to the small embankment, the car door flew open and 'Devil' broke into a run across the sandy beach. Nicole ran after her while Gabriel took off above the beach on the embankment, running parallel to them both. It was difficult running in the sand, but 'Devil' was making good time. Nicole struggled to keep up, slowly losing ground. There was a problem approaching 'Devil'. At the end of the beach stood large, jagged boulders stacked up. She was forced to turn and head up the embankment to return to solid ground. Just as she came over the lip of the embankment, Gabriel tackled her.

'Devil' twisted and writhed violently, trying to break free. Gabriel took a few hits just trying to pin the woman down. If Nicole had been any slower, the woman may have been able to get away. Gabriel was losing the battle to hold her in place, despite his superior strength. But when Nicole jumped on top of the woman and cuffed her, the fighting ended.

Gabriel stood, rubbing his chin. Nicole kept her knee in the woman's back and looked up at him. All three people, exhausted from the ordeal, struggled to catch their breath.

Nicole smiled, and between breaths said, "She's almost as hard to hang onto as a slippery pike!"

Gabriel burst into laughter, along with Nicole. 'Devil' only scowled as she lay on the ground, defeated. After a short victory laugh, they walked the woman to their car and tossed her onto the backseat. Nicole was grateful that Justin had been able to bring an unmarked police car so she could safely stow their prisoner in the back.

"This isn't over. You will pay…one way or another," threatened the woman.

Nicole just slammed the door on her.

"Now what?" inquired Gabriel.

"Now I should try finding someone who can help. Probably, it's only our area that has corruption in the Force. I think I'll call headquarters and hopefully they'll believe me."

CHAPTER 19

Officer Henry Jackson had just settled in for his morning shift at OPP headquarters near Toronto. It had been a beautiful morning, and he hoped for a calm day at the office. When he received the message there was an officer calling from the Fort Frances detachment, he thought that was odd. It was rather isolated and usually fairly quiet over there. No one ever called headquarters from that area.

"Jackson here," was his curt answer to the phone call.

"Hello sir. This is Constable Nicole Edouard. I have a very strange story to tell you. And I need your help."

"Ok…" he responded hesitantly. "Go ahead."

Nicole detailed all of the events that took place over the previous few days. Henry just listened silently. When she finished, he was at a loss for words. This was the most astonishing development he had ever heard! Could it all be true? Surely, no one could make all of this up. And why would they? A long pause ensued while he tried to process this.

He took a drink of water while Nicole awaited his response.

"Sir? Are you still there?" she finally asked.

"Yes. I'm going to have to put you on hold for a moment."

Henry took the break to decide what to do. After he thought about the issues involved with corruption at the detachment, the active scene at the mine, and the fact they were holding a prisoner, he decided to take decisive action.

"Edouard, I'll be sending help your way immediately. Hang on for a couple hours," he told Nicole.

"I will sir," she responded.

Henry hoped he was making the right decision. He picked up the phone and ordered a plane be chartered immediately. Next, he recruited a group of officers to join him on the flight. It would probably take them three hours to fly there, but he wasn't going to entrust a situation like this to anyone else. He would personally handle this. Next, he called for a helicopter to be brought into Fort Frances from a nearby detachment. Then he drove to the airport. So much for a quiet morning.

*   *   *

Justin awoke to the sound of sirens coming down the long, winding driveway at Gabriel's. He looked around him and called out, with no answer. Where were Gabriel and Nicole? Confused, Justin tried to sit up and winced from the pain. He took a breath and tried to stand, but fell back down on the couch crying from the pain. Then he heard a couple vehicles brake hard just outside and people approach the door.

"Bang…bang…bang," came the sound of someone pounding on the door. "Justin! Are you in there?"

"Yeah. I can't move," was his answer.

The door swung open and two officers stormed in - guns at the ready. They swept through the house, checking every corner. Two paramedics crept in behind them and came to check on Justin when they saw him. They began looking him over, paying special attention to his wounded leg.

"It's ok. We're here to help," one of them spoke reassuringly.

"All clear!" shouted an officer. "Well, hello Constable. How are you feeling?" he asked Justin.

"Umm. Ok. In agony," was his reply. "Who are you? How did you find me?"

"We're the reinforcements. Your friend Edouard called us in. Your nightmare should be over now."

"Thank God! Where is she? Where's Gabriel? Are they ok?" Justin asked with intensity.

"They're fine. In fact, I think they're leading a team on a raid right now…"

*　　*　　*

As Justin was receiving help, Nicole and Gabriel landed at the dock on the island with a team of officers. They lead them to the cave and revealed the immense wealth inside. Nothing had been touched. Dylan's body still lay there, and they found the other two bodies at the back as well. It appeared that no one had returned to the cave yet. The group of officers started preparing to transport the bodies out. Nicole and Gabriel stood outside on the dock to watch the proceedings.

"What will happen to all that gold?" Gabriel asked.

"It's an active crime scene right now, so it will all be catalogued and held for the time being. I don't know what they'll do with it after," Nicole answered.

"I guess I should get my boat. It's still parked on the other side of the island."

"I'll go with you," Nicole offered.

While they were walking, a helicopter flew overheard. They looked up and watched as it flew in the direction of Longhorn Point. As they neared the spot Gabriel had marked on a map for them, the officers looked down to see an active excavation on the ground. There were a few guys hanging around the hole staring up at them.

"Stay where you are!" ordered an officer from the helicopter. "This is the police!"

Everyone on the ground scattered to escape. A few stragglers poured out of the mine and ran toward the boats. However, each of them encountered a team of officers on the ground, ready to pounce. All the men were cuffed and held, while a couple officers checked out the mine to ensure no one was hiding in there. The whole operation was mopped up before day's end.

CHAPTER 20

"Secret Gold Mining Conspiracy Discovered!" The day after shutting down the mine operation, this headline appeared in news articles across North America, mentioning the few details that had been released. A man sat in his office reading the story while puffing on a cigar. He sat back puffing away when his phone rang.

"Yes?" was his gruff answer. "I saw the story just now…No, I didn't see this coming either. It appears our operations manager there didn't fully apprise us of her problems. Let's not panic yet. If we're patient, we can probably recover some things. In the meantime, we'll carry on with our other operations. One day…we'll set things right."

*   *   *

Back in Fort Frances, Nicole exited the police station along with Gabriel. They finally finished giving their detailed statements to Henry Jackson. All the conspirators were in custody, including 'Devil'. They hadn't figured out her real name yet. The whole detachment would be examined for any other possible partners with Jack Rudiger. Nicole would receive commendation for her role in exposing everything. They happily extended some paid vacation time to her. And Gabriel was offered an award, which he refused. He had expressed appreciation, but did not wish to be publicly recognized.

"I can't believe it's finally over," Gabriel said with a sigh.

"I know. I'm so glad it's done!" Nicole replied. "It'll be nice to take a couple weeks off to recover."

"What will you do with your time off?" he inquired.

Nicole stopped and looked at him with a smile. "I was thinking it would be a good time to practice my cast. Know anyone who could help me with that?"

She gave him a playful push and giggled, walking further down the street. Gabriel stood with a satisfied smile as he watched her walk away. Though this had been the most horrible mess to go through, in this moment…it was all worth it…to have her.

Nicole turned around and smiled affectionately at him.

"Come on, Gabriel. Let's get something to eat," she invited.

He jogged to catch up and she slipped her hand in his, pulling herself toward him as they headed to the cafe down the street.

THE END

Manufactured by Amazon.ca
Acheson, AB

15152162R00129